BELLA'S PACT

BY
PHILLIP TUCKER

www.philliptucker.com.au

ACKNOWLEDGEMENT

To my family and friends. As long as a man has both, he is truly blessed. Thanks to all of you for your support. A special thanks to Steven and Dianne.

CONTENTS

EPILOGUE

I was working a late shift in the Emergency Department of the hospital on a Friday night when a skinny young woman of eighteen was admitted. She'd overdosed on Ice, a rather nasty cheap drug available in the local area. Placed in critical care, she was in a bad state, coming down hard off the stuff. In the end, they were forced to defibrillate her, to stabilise her heart, bring her back from near death.

For the next hour she appeared comatose, only the monitors on the wall above her, showed she was still with us. During this time, I helped the nurses wash the filth and vomit from her body, tossing away the soiled clothing she was wearing. The nurses worried for her took turns sitting with her. One even combed her hair. Lying there, dressed in a white hospital gown, she looked like an angel resting.

Clean, she was pretty, with long flowing brown curly hair. She reminded me of one of the elves of Lord of the Rings, having their oval-shaped face and deep blue eyes. Her only imperfection was her overly thin body. 'Feeding the needle' they called this look, one of the many side effects of drug abuse. If you had entered the ED at that moment, you'd have thought she was just a young woman sleeping, not a care in the world, a far cry from the reality.

As the department became swamped with new arrivals, the nurses being stretched to the limit asked me to sit with her and hold her hand.

"No one dies alone" she whispered to me, moving away. Since working in the ED, I found this golden rule was something special to our nurses. They always where possible, hold the hand of a patient who may pass away in the absence of a loved one. It communicated to the person, in their final moments that someone cared. I've only had to do this once before, and I can assure you, the experience stays with you forever.

Holding her hand, I sat there silently, watching the nurses and doctors frantically deal with situations, which to the everyday person would be overwhelming. The work they do is both emotionally and physically demanding. I often wonder how their personal lives are affected by working in this trauma filled environment.

A slight tug on my hand made me look down to see the young woman was awake. Shame, fear, anger and confusion were some of the emotions, which usually erupted to the surface when a drug user wakes up in hospital. This can be followed by the person's delusional violence, attacking anyone in reach or the compulsion to flee. Instead, she just lay there watching me, as if determining what type of person I was.

Asking someone 'how they are' in the hospital seems lame, but it was the only thing I could think of, expecting an entirely different reaction from her. She didn't answer; she just gave a small smile. Her eyes then shifted towards a bottle of water sitting on a tray next to her bed. Getting permission from a relieved nurse, I gave her a drink through a straw, holding the bottle. She drank about a third, before signalling with a shake of her head that she had enough.

"I'm still here?" she croaked out, finding her voice.

"Yes, though you scared the Doctor."

"I'd planned to move on." She replied still with that small smile on her face. Perplexed not knowing what to say, I just sat there, in the end, I had to ask the obvious.

"Why?"

She started hesitantly then grew in confidence, telling me her story. Unburdening can sometimes free a person of their troubles; in her case, I wasn't sure.

She'd been abused at a young age, thrown out of home. Although she didn't say what had occurred, I could see by her facial expression, it was something horrendous. Living on the streets, she'd eked out an existence, doing odd jobs, while she travelled around. Falling in with three friends, they'd got a place together, forming something resembling normality. Drugs and sex were a big part of their culture, a way of forgetting, she told me.

One night, after several drinks at a bar, she'd been taken outside and brutally raped by two men. Left in a horrific state in a back lane, she was discovered by a young couple taking a shortcut home. Calling an ambulance, the couple stayed with her, till it arrived. Telling the paramedics how they'd found her, they swiftly carried out emergency first aid, stabilising her, before transporting her to the local hospital.

Waking up the next day after undergoing minor surgery, the doctor assured her she'd be okay. He also told her that the police had been informed of the sexual assault. Asking her if she was up for them to interview her, she agreed. Getting her okay, he immediately called the police.

When the police arrived, they seemed genuinely upset by her condition, believing her. Giving a description of the men, she could see the cops look at one another. They knew the two men. They were supposedly upright members of the community and both married. Taking her statement, they promised to get back to her. The doctor seeing them leaving, gave them semen samples and DNA evidence taken from her when she was brought in. Thanking him, they then hastily left.

After two weeks and hearing nothing, she went to the police station. Even though surveillance tapes at the bar confirmed they'd left with her, the police wouldn't pursue the case. It was pointed out to her, that in court, a lowlife druggie's word wasn't worth anything, against two people of good character. Suggesting it might be better if she left town, the cops considering the matter closed, moved on. She'd recently stopped using, following this episode, she returned to her habit.

Telling her friends what had happened didn't seem to surprise them. All had problems, and no one cared. At a low point in the conversation, one of her companions opted to end her own life, when the time was right, as she put it. Jokingly the others made a pact to carry through on ending their lives if the pain of living became too great. When she finished her story, I didn't know what to say. I lived a relatively normal life, with a loving wife and kids. Her life to mine was like being a beggar in a third world country to a Hollywood movie star. I tried to point out that life was worth living that she could change her situation and be happy. She didn't answer she just stared at me.

My phone ringing ended my time with her. A problem had arisen in the General Ward, needing my presence. Promising to come back I left, as a nurse resumed watching over her in my stead. When I returned, she was gone, having walked out of the hospital, dressed only in a white gown. I never saw her again, and I hope she made it, though I have my doubts. The world is a cruel place for the less fortunate; this book is for that young woman whose name I never bothered to find out.

When I checked later, I found she'd used a fake surname and the letter B for her name. I chose Bella.

NEW YEARS EVE 1996

Byron Bay was pumping. New Year's Eve was going to go off, and Jenny wasn't going to miss out. Everybody who was somebody was going to be at the party at the clubhouse. Not to be there, just wasn't part of her thinking. Having finished her first year at University, she was home for the summer break. Needing to earn some much-needed money for the next year, she'd taken a part-time job in a local clothing boutique.

Deciding to let her hair down and have some fun, she rang several of her girlfriends, arranging to meet them there. From one she learned that an old heartthrob of hers from high school was going to be there. Considering the possibility of hooking up with him, she splurged on a tight-fitting brief outfit, to show him she still had it. The problem was, her father was a stick in the mud, always warning her of the dangers of going to the Bay.

Being over 18 now gave her a sense of empowerment. So when she told her parents where she was going, she made it clear she didn't want any shit from them. Getting a 'you're still our daughter look' from them both, she promised to behave and ring them if she drank too much. The dress she left home wearing, wasn't the dress she bought to wear that night. This one was to appease the parents that she was at least wearing a decent outfit.

A couple of clicks short of the Byron Bay township she parked her car behind an old kombi. Seeing parking any closer to town wasn't going happen, she moved around to the passenger side of the vehicle. Removing her dress, she stripped down to her G-string and bra on the side the road. Getting several honks from passing motorists, she blew several kisses, before putting on her party dress. Many of those passing motorists would've wondered why she'd park so far from the town she smiled, knowing it was the sensible thing to do if you knew Byron Bay.

Parking miles away from the town, before dressing and walking, was Bay logic at its best. Locals knew that you couldn't park anywhere near the town itself, so rather than get angry you adapted and use your feet. Looking towards the village in the distance, she saw a never-ending line of parked cars parked bumper to bumper, on both sides of the road. 'They are doing exactly what I've done' she mused; meaning tonight was going to be huge with a large sprinkling of locals. Anticipating this situation, she grabbed her running shoes from under the seat of the car, putting them on. Knowing she was over two kilometre's from the town, she moved off, setting a good pace, looking forward to the night.

As expected, the surf club was packed to the rafters. Chuckling, Jenny walked past it; locals knew the real action was on the beach. She was amazed at the size of the crowd gathered there, it was standing room only. Letting herself go, she joined in, dancing and singing along with the music. Weaving her way through the tight-knit crowd along the beach, she enjoyed herself, looking for her friends. Stopping when the mood took her, she rubbed her stuff up against a nice assortment of young hard bodies.

They all tried to score with her, but she kept moving, giving them the 'maybe later' line, and her trademark smile. Hearing her name screamed above the music, she looked towards the surf, locating her friends waving wildly. Rushing through the crowd to them, they all ended up in a pile on the sand, hugging each other laughing hysterically.

Joining them, catching up, she had in no time, downed several cocktails full of a mixture of spirits and 'pick me up' pills. Like an earthquake, the rush hit her, as she let the music flow over her, letting herself go. Swaying to the music with her friends, she checked out the crowd. She noticed several guys paying close attention to her moves, appraising her appearance. They obviously liked what they were seeing, as she rolled her hips, giving them a sneak peck at what she had.

Jenny knew she looked sensational tonight. Blessed with long mousey blonde hair and an angelic blemish-free face, made her above average. Backed up with a tight firm body, a good set of perky breasts made her irresistible. These in themselves would get her any guy there, but they weren't her winning assets. "Legs" the boys had called her at High school, pointing out, how her legs went right up to her armpits, they were so long. Athletics at school was the reason; running in cross-country races had made them what they were today. Tonight with her tight body-hugging dress, she let them look, teasing them, promising them pleasures beyond their dreams.

She wasn't the only one strutting her stuff that night; there were hundreds of girls on the beach doing their best to drive the men crazy. Her friends famous for their prick teasing were on fire tonight. Their dance became a series of seductive flowing movements, orchestrated down to the tiniest detail, to drive the watching men to the brink. Mesmerized by the show, they competed with each other, for the chance to have one magical dance with any of these temptresses. 'Moths to the flame' Jenny smiled watching a never-ending parade of men try to win them over.

Flexing their muscles and strutting their stuff, they tried every move they had to hook up with one of her sought-after friends, before the coming New Year's celebration. Jenny smiling secretly admitted to herself that more than a few impressed her. She was just about to give one the green light when on queue, her old flame materialised from the throng. He promptly made his move, rubbing up against her arse, showing her what he had. Laughing she let him pull her to him, as he kissed her, thrusting his tongue into her mouth.

Pushing into his crotch with her sex, she rubbed him up and down. His smile was soon replaced with a look of pure lust as he enjoyed the trip down memory lane. Feeling the swelling start, she danced away smiling, having reminded him of what she could do. When he tried for a quick feel, she pushed him away fainting surprise at his unprovoked intimacy.

"Maybe later." She told him giggling, moving on, having proved her point. Her ex-dismissed, danced away into the crowd his ego deflated, as he searched for another partner. Taking a break with her friends, they all went hysterical, as Jenny told them tales of conquest and letdowns, while she'd been at University. They, in turn, brought her up to speed with what had been going on locally, as the booze continued to flow.

Seeing that the time was climbing towards midnight, her group joined the dance, all looking for partners for midnight. Solo now; Jenny wove her way again through the crowd, looking for a partner to share the upcoming celebrations, someone special. Her high school heartthrob she found passed out on the sand. Two stone-faced unimpressed paramedics were preparing to move him away from the beach, to a waiting ambulance.

Laughing, thinking it was all a joke, she looked around seeing a good-looking guy watching her from the balcony of the clubhouse. It only took a thrust of her hips to the music, and he was down beside her, up close and friendly. Pulling her roughly to him, his hands gripping her arse, he shoved his tongue into her mouth, as the countdown started. The guy was a smoker, turning her off, making her push him away unimpressed. Getting a 'fuck you' from him, he moved off, as New Year's Eve erupted around her.

A hand on her shoulder made her turn. A good-looking guy stood there, he timidly asked for a kiss for the New Years. Laughing she grabbed him, thrusting her tongue into his mouth. 'Guy must be a virgin,' she mused, feeling his lower body spring to attention at her aggressiveness. Forgetting her friends, she took the virgin's hand, not remembering if he'd told her his name, leading him out into the darkness of the beach, away from the crowd.

Dropping onto the sand with her new man, they groped their way through foreplay, before going at it like wild animals. They screwed each other's brains out for the next 40 minutes before Jenny decided to call it a night. Satisfied, giving the guy 'you're the best ever' line, she tried to find her friends. They were long gone, having found their own partners for the darkness. Spent, and coming down from her high, Jenny decided to call it a night.

She knew she was beyond driving, so rather than risk getting caught by the cops or slamming into a pole, she opted to sleep in her car. Putting on her running shoes, she began the long walk back to her car. The roads in the town itself were packed with guys hanging out of car windows. Wolf whistling and honking their horns as they drove past her, only one thing on their minds. Smiling, she did her best to drive them wild, putting on a show swaying her butt, as she walked along. Many stopped offering her a lift, but there was no way she was getting into a car, with a wild bunch of horny guys.

"What a night!" She laughed, spotting the edge of the town and in the distance, her car. She figured that once she left the town she had about a kilometre to walk.

Most of the cars were gone by now, with only the odd one every now and then. They sat there like neglected toys by the side of the road, waiting and hoping that their owners returned. Leaving the town outskirts, the footpath, which stood between the road and wall-to-wall units, changed. The road still bordered one side; the other now faced dense bushland. Usually, the dark didn't bother her, but earlier that week, she'd had an incident at work.

She'd been doing a stock-take after closing time, in the office at the rear of the shop. The owner had gone to fetch them both something to eat, leaving her to continue checking the accounts. Concentrating on her ledger entries, she'd seen a flash of movement near the rear window of the shop beside her. Even though the window and doors were barred, it had made her jump, frightening her. Scared, feeling someone was out there watching her; she'd run to the front of the shop unsure what to do.

The owner returned a few minutes later to find Jenny standing in the middle of the shop quivering with fear. Bordering on hysteria, she tried to explain what had occurred. Animatedly she'd told him of seeing a blur of movement, which maybe had been a person, but could've been anything. Picking up a baseball bat kept in the shop in case of trouble, her boss opened the rear door, checking outside with a torch. Having a good look around and finding nothing, he assured her she was safe.

Calming down, the two of them ate their meals silently, before both spontaneously bursting into laughter. Putting it down to overworking and nerves, her boss just the same to be safe, had run her home. Thanking him and apologising for all the trouble, she went to bed that night feeling a complete idiot. By the next day, she'd moved on, forgetting about it putting it down to stress. Now as she stared into the bushes, her fear of that night returned.

Increasing her pace, she walked silently along, as the bush seemed to close in on the path. The feeling of being watched made her stop and think about walking back to the safety of the built-up area. Laughing at herself, she walked on with renewed determination, steeling herself against her own frailty. A noise behind her made her turn. There in the dim light silhouetted by the urban glow, a shadow moved along the path behind her.

As if sensing she'd seen it, the shadow seemed to freeze, watching her, before casually merging with the undergrowth like some malevolent apparition. Now gone, Jenny blinking, was left wondering if she'd real seen anything, or it was just the booze. The sound of branches breaking underfoot as it continued in her direction ended her doubts, as terrified, she screamed and started running.

Having covered half the distance to her car, she ground to a halt winded, as the effect of too much booze and drugs stole her vigour. Breathing heavily, gasping for breath, she hesitantly, looked towards the mocking safety of the suburbs.

"Where the fuck, are all the cars?" She cried out, knowing how busy this road usually was. The sound of breaking branches brought her back to reality.

Someone or something was still pursuing her through the undergrowth. Her escalating panic produced more adrenalin, giving her renewed strength. Turning back towards her car, she propelled herself towards its safety. Jogging this time, controlling her running as she had during marathons, she knew she could make it. This was what she was good at, she told herself. Regaining her confidence, she pushed herself towards the safety of her car.

A couple of spaces behind her car stood an old brown van. The side door was open, and a guy stood next to it, loading a spare tyre into the back of his vehicle.

"Help me!" She screamed out, rushing into the surprised man's arms, as breathing heavily; she tried to pull herself together. The man, in turn, wrapped his arms around her comforting her.

"Take it easy. What's the problem?" He asked, holding her.

"Sorry I didn't mean to scare you, but someone's after me." She stammered out, as the man looked past her, searching for danger.

"I can't see anybody are you sure?" He asked still holding her. Jenny at first was too frightened to look back. Overcoming her fear, feeling safe with the man's support, she turned around. Standing there right in front of her was a man dressed in black. Breathing heavily, his face frozen with a crazy, frightening sneer, he moved towards her. Shocked, she looked at the man holding her, to see the same sneer on his face.

"We've got you now plaything." He giggled, his free hand roving over her thighs. Shoving the man away, she made a dash for her car, as a rope seemed to jump of its own accord around her neck. Putting her hands to her throat to try and release it and scream, she felt the man in black grab her from behind. As both men grappled with her, dragging her towards the open side door, she felt the rope around her neck tighten, making her gasp for breath.

The two men now pushed her inside the van, securing her hands. Loosening the noose around her throat, a rag was then shoved into her mouth. The sound of horns honking as cars drove by, spurred Jenny to action. Kicking out, knowing she was fighting for her life, she frantically waved two-handed, out the side window, hoping a passing car would see her struggling. Several punches to her stomach took the resistance out of her, as she collapsed onto the floor.

Lying in pain just conscious, she heard her captors laugh insanely, as her legs were tied together. The man dressed in black, seeing she was secure, climbed over the front seat, starting the van. Erupting into life, the vehicle accelerated down the road, as the tyre changer in the back with her, produced a knife. Cringing back, she watched him come towards her, expertly cutting off her dress and underclothes. Terrified beyond belief, she lay whimpering on the floor, as the man stood above her, silently looking down at her.

"You'll remember this night for the rest of your life." He told her, his voice charged with emotion, his sexual arousal evident, as he stood over her. Chuckling at her fear, he climbed over the seat, joining his friend, leaving her on the floor in the dark.

Jenny lay there, trembling with fear. She knew she was in deep shit. If they were just going to fuck her, they'd have done it by now. Her imagination was running wild; terror was taking hold, at the prospect of what lay ahead. Frantically she yanked and twisted on her bindings, trying to loosen the ropes securing her hands. The pain as the ropes cut made her scream silently behind the gag, as she continued to try and break free. Panic seised as her as she found the ropes had no give in them at all. By the time the van stopped at its destination, she had given up hope of getting free. Looking up towards the front, she saw the two men staring at her.

"She'll be the best yet, look at those legs!" The man pretending to change the tyre sniggered, making her wet herself in terror.

At any other time, she'd have found these men attractive, though slightly older than the men she usually preferred, but not now. Though both men were nice-looking, there was something feral in the way they looked at her. It was as if she was just a piece of meat, which they intended to be carved up between them. Shuddering with dread, she watched them jump out of the van, opening the side door. As they dragged her out, she continued to resist, kicking out wildly with her bound feet trying her best to stop them. Laughing, one grabbed her right breast, viciously squeezing it, making her groan in agony.

The other with a professional air about him shoved a needle into her arm. Subdued, the drugs taking effect, they loaded her into an old wheelbarrow. As one pushed her towards an old farmhouse, the other watched her hungrily, making her sob, as horror replaced fear. By the time they'd reached the house the drugs had overwhelmed her system, her world had become surreal. Jenny's mind struggled to comprehend her situation.

Taking her to a large bed, they secured her hands removing her gag. One of the men then stripped as the other walked to a camera facing it towards her. The first man pulled her legs apart and brutally entered her. Whatever the drug was they'd given her, it didn't inhibit the pain, as her ordeal began. At first, she thought it better to let him have his fun, not resisting, it was the wrong decision. Climbing off her, seeing her lying there, submitting, he brutally beat her with a small whip, till she screamed in agony at every touch.

"That's it plaything you scream all you want." He chuckled, as pulling her legs apart again, he continued his rape. His partner, laughing insanely encouraged him, suggesting different things to try, as he manoeuvered the camera around the bed. Sobbing with terror and unimaginable pain, Jenny watched her rapist suddenly tense. With a satisfied groan of pleasure he came.

Crawling off her, both tired and exhilarated from his fun, the man told his partner to take his place. Eagerly he handed the camera to his partner, before tearing off his clothes and moving towards her. Screaming or pleading only inspired them to continue finding new ways to cause her pain. Although Jenny was reduced to a blood-covered pulp, she continued to fight for life, crying out for help.

"Daddy help me!" She screamed over and over again, hoping for a miracle, that he would hear her cries and rescue her. The man in black sat on the bed beside her, listening to her cries, running his hands over her once beautiful body, giggling softly.

"Daddy's not going to help you tonight plaything." He chuckled, as across the room, the phone in her bag they'd brought in the barrow with her, started to ring. Both men seemed momentarily surprised by the ringing. The fake tyre changer, manning the camera dropped it onto a table, rushing to the bag. Taking out the phone, he smashed it on the ground, his eyes wild with excitement. He was just about to return to the camera when he saw a photo in her handbag.

It was a picture of Jenny and her parents, taken at her eighteenth birthday. What made him stare was her father was dressed in his police uniform. Showing it to his friend the grin left his face. Jenny watched them both come towards her; knowing screaming was a waste of time. Still, she screamed anyway, as they placed the rope back around her neck. Together they slowly pulled it, tighter and tighter, watching her gasp for breath, till she gave up her forlorn fight for life.

"What a waste. I was so looking forward to revisiting our new plaything in the future." The tyre changer chuckled, as the other looked down at their handy work.

"I know my friend, but this one's father would definitely look for us. Better to leave him guessing." He pointed out, pushing the body back into the wheelbarrow.

"Do you think we'll have any trouble?" This made his friend hesitate. Letting go of the wheelbarrow, he sat down beside him.

"Maybe, I wouldn't think so though. But I think we should stop using the van, I always thought it was a bit too obvious."

"It served us well though. We've caught a few playthings with it." The man in black smiled.

"Yes, but now it's time to move on my friend, I've got a much better idea to try." The tyre changer sniggered.

PRESENT DAY THE MONTH OF MARCH 2012

The elderly couple hand in hand, walked from their car to the lookout, without a word being spoken. The enforced silence had nothing to do with their relationship; it was out of respect for what had occurred here in the past. Groaning slightly, Dave slowed, to let his legs warm up, after spending so much time sitting. It made him angry that his once indestructible body had betrayed him, surrendering to old age. It forced him to creep along, while before in his younger days, he would've walked effortlessly, enjoying every minute.

Nearing the popular tourist spot, Dave stopped to gaze across the valley to the falls in the distance. It never failed to impress the once hardened detective of the NSW Police Force, with its spellbinding beauty. For over thirty years he'd dished out rough justice to lawbreakers, mostly in the North Coast region of NSW. Now he sat silently clutching his wife's hand, his eyes glistened as a tear escaped. Travelling down his aged cheek, it reached his upper lip before he hastily wiped the sign of his emotional weakness away.

Ten years it had been to the day, when he'd come here for quite a different reason, as flashes of that day flooded his mind, torturing his soul. In the distance unaffected by his emotions, the waterfall continued to gush from the valley wall. Halting to look at the view and taking a breather, Dave Johnson and his wife Helen, sat down on a bench at the lookout. Even at this distance, he could feel the mind-numbing roar from the falls. It seemed to reverberate through his chest, as the water tried unendingly to crush the granite rocks in the valley below.

"God forgive me!" He unknowingly said out loud, as his wife beside him squeezed his hand, comforting him.

"You were just doing your job love. There's nothing you could've done." Helen whispered, trying to ease his pain.

"And look how many lives it cost!" Dave groaned, remembering the sound of those screams.

MARCH 2002

The four young friends slowly ambled along the disused railway track, heading north. No one spoke, as they shared a quiet moment, enjoying the security of companionship. They didn't have to babble on trying to impress each other. The four friends loved the others unconditionally, and this needed no words.

Jed, the more wired of the three, found walking in silence hard to take. He amused himself, by kicking the odd can or throwing rocks at the many rusted signs. The disused railway line provided plenty of rocks to vent his frustrations. The others watched his antics with a mixture of happiness and hidden sadness, knowing the reason for his inability to relax.

They'd all been close friends since primary school, bonding into a tight-knit group, drawn together for a variety of reasons, supporting each other. Life had not been easy for any of them. Though their family's social standing and lifestyles were different in every way, they were bonded to each other by an emotional need that transcended all boundaries.

"How much further is it?" Jed asked, breaking the imposed silence.

"It's not far to the turn-off, you'll make it," Michael replied, trying to conceal a slight smile on the corner of his lips. Jed was famous for his fitness, or more accurately, his total lack of it. Kirra, in front, turned smiling. Her smile had always been able to brighten the day.

"Weren't you the one Jed, who first brought us on this walk to the falls?" She giggled. Her mood was infectious, and the others couldn't help smiling.

"Well, it's been awhile," Jed answered defensively, making the others laugh at his roundabout confession. Kirra turning back around increased her pace slightly, catching up to Bella. The girls resumed their conversation, talking among themselves, enjoying the others company. Michael behind them playfully grabbed Jed, ruffling his hair, as they continued walking.

Rounding a bend, they glimpsed the start of the walking track that would take them up into the hills. As one, they all cheered, knowing they'd reached the best part of the walk. Leaving the monotony of the flat railway line, they started their ascent into the hills. It wasn't the most ideal day for a hike up into the mountains, Michael thought, as he looked at the gloomy grey sky. It had been like this since they started, threatening rain, choking the sunlight. 'Well, at least it's warm' he smiled, knowing this area of the North Coast of NSW, was always warm regardless of the season.

Moving further into the hills, Michael watched as the surrounding countryside changed, from light scrub with patches of farmland, to dense rainforest. The track seemed to wind right through the heart of the forest, giving the four a brief taste of how magnificent it had once been. Michael, recalled, how once the forest had covered the entire area, an impenetrable barrier, a set of lungs for the planet. Then man and his machines had arrived, destroying everything beautiful in his path, ploughing nature under. Now only scattered remnants survived, a small reminder of what once had been.

"At least I helped save some of it," Michael whispered to himself, remembering the heady days of the forest protest movement.

Coming back to the present, Michael focused on the two girls in front of him. They walked side-by-side holding hands, chatting merrily. His heart pumped harder at just being with them, as his eyes were drawn to the roll of their hips, tantalising him. Jed beside him also felt the hypnotic pull the two women exerted on the men.

Following behind, each young man felt, as if some mythical siren in an ancient fable was drawing him along.

Bella was on the left and had a boyish, athletic figure. She walked effortlessly along, her body enjoying every step. She wasn't stunningly beautiful, but she was pretty. Bella was the type of girl that a shy boy could sit down with and start up a conversation, knowing she would not ridicule him, but support him. She had a gift for seeing the good side of people.

Beside her, Kirra with her full hourglass figure strolled along. She was stunningly beautiful, although she went to great lengths to hide it. She'd been both blessed and cursed with eye-catching good looks. Since school, she had always attracted attention from the opposite sex, mostly unwanted. She could've had any boy she wanted; instead, she'd chosen Jed and Michael. Somehow she knew they loved her for who she was, not what they could get from her. She too seemed to be enjoying the walking, although she was breathing heavily on the steep rises.

Each girl wore a loose-fitting rainbow coloured dress, giving them free movement. Maybe not the best clothing for hiking, but today was special, so they'd worn their favourites. On their feet, they wore boots suitable for bushwalking, though they would have preferred to go barefoot. The problem for the boys was that the girls wore nothing underneath their dresses. As their bodies perspired, their clothing became near transparent, sticking to the contours of their bodies. This caused Michael and Jed to concentrate more on the girls, than where their feet were landing.

Michael over the years had made love to both Kirra and Bella, as had Jed. They were continually changing partners, never becoming jealous or attached to just one companion. Their love for each other as a group was always their driving emotion, an unbreakable bond. Many of their friends outside of their group, had trouble with their incestuous relationship. They weren't upset by this, knowing what they had, was unique, somehow spiritual.

To them, sex was a celebration of their relationship; it somehow consummated the four into a family. Love had become like breathing to them, something they needed to do to survive, a way to hide their pain. In time the track widened into an old fire trail. The boys moved up, walking beside the girls on the outer edges, holding the hand of the girl inside of them. Even this small show of affection, triggered a spontaneous smile from each of them as if electricity was flowing from one person to the others.

Walking further into the mountains, the track became steeper, pushing the four as if trying to stop them from reaching their destination. Jed, struggling for breath stopped. Bending over in pain, he vomited onto the track. Michael beside him swiftly reached out, holding his friend, until he steadied. Recovered enough to stand on his own, Jed shaking badly, frantically searched his backpack.

Finding a small plastic bag filled with pills, Jed grabbed several, dropping them into his mouth, before swallowing a mouthful of water from his bottle. His three friends silently watched him. Pity was written on their faces, as Jed recovering, signalled that he was alright.

"Those pills own you, Jed!" Michael scolded him, angry at his situation.

"You're right mate, I can't live without them," Jed confessed sadly, as Michael reached across pulling his friend into a bear hug, trying to share his grief. Jed self-conscious of his friend's sentiment for him broke the embrace. Smiling at the others, assuring them he was ready to move on, he shuffled forward. Hesitantly the others resumed the walk, though all of them watched Jed more closely.

Kirra and Bella felt Jed's pain in a way Michael couldn't. They too had been hooked on Ice. Unlike Jed, they'd managed to wrestle free, when first addicted to the drug, mostly through his help. Now Jed only functioned by taking a steady stream of the tablets. They no longer gave him the high he'd craved; now they just kept him alive. This had caused Jed another problem, as his supplier knew he was hooked. Continually raising the price, Jed had no choice but to pay or die.

A tear dropped from Jed's eyes unnoticed by the others, as he trudged along, doing his best to keep pace with them. He'd once been a football star, destined to represent the country. Back in his early teens, he weighed in at over ninety kilo's, mostly muscle. Now he weighed close to fifty wringing wet, a skeleton of his former self. That was all before these small insignificant pills had come along, brightening his day.

Michael beside him pretended not to notice his friend's tears. With all the problems he'd had in his life, drugs luckily hadn't been one of them. He had a wafer-thin body but had always been that way, never having much weight to throw around. He owed his lean physic to his early childhood with his family, 'if you could call it that', he thought angrily. Knowing thinking about the past wouldn't help, he let it go, concentrating on walking.

Reaching the top of the plateau, the group located a break in the tree canopy, where the sun had broken through, producing a grass-covered meadow. Crashing to the ground, the group pulled out water bottles, drinking deeply. Lying down on their backs, they rested, watching the clouds break up above them.

"Not far to go now!" Kirra smiled, stretching like a cat, practically purring at being able to rest.

"About twenty minutes to the waterhole, then another ten to the falls," Jed informed them, as his eyes wandered along Bella's long smooth legs, as she lay next to him. She didn't talk as much as she once had he thought sadly. In the early days, she would excitedly converse on any subject, going on for hours. Sometimes she would stop only when she found the others had all gone to sleep, 'that was Bella', which made him smile.

He longed for those times, as his smile slowly retreated remembering why she had changed. As if sensing his thoughts, she reached across touching his arm, giving him a rare smile. 'Bella the Saint' he'd called her. Always trusting, never seeing the dark side of people, it had been her downfall.

Michael sitting next to the sleeping Kirra, ran his hand along her thigh to where her dress had ridden up while she rested. Looking at her face, he saw a smile appear on her lips, as her eyes flickered open, watching him. She knew what he wanted; her thighs slowly undulating enjoying his touch.

"Let's wait till the waterhole Michael." She whispered, stretching like a cat, her voice full of promise. 'It will be better there once we've refreshed ourselves." She smiled, her hand squeezing the front of his pants playfully. Michael in response leapt to his feet.

"In that case, let's get going then." He beckoned to the others to follow, as he moved back to the track. Catching his enthusiasm, his three companions rose from the ground, following his lead, shaking off their fatigue. Michael knew he'd always been the leader of this dysfunctional group. He hadn't wanted to, it had just happened. Something to do with his childhood, he guessed.

MICHAEL

When Michael was five years old, he remembered waiting with his older brothers, who were twelve and fourteen to meet his father. Their mother had told them their father had been away with the government, for seven years, doing secret work. His older brothers knew the truth; their father had been in prison for robbing banks. Their father was known as a career criminal. In other words, he got caught a lot.

Born during the depression, he blamed everyone for his lack of employment, leading to his lifetime of crime. Many at the time knew this was just a lie. The man had plenty of jobs, his problem was, he had a bad temper when drunk and enjoyed inflicting pain. Of course, working a forty-hour week for bosses who expected you to turn up on time and frowned on fighting, didn't sit well with him.

Stealing and robbing he found were two things he liked doing, this fitted into the lifestyle he wanted, with the bonus of being able to inflict pain. Unfortunately, he wasn't a smart criminal, being regularly caught. From showing his face during the robbery to shooting his mouth off when drunk, somehow he always ended up back inside.

There was another problem for Michael that his brothers had snidely hinted at. By rights, he shouldn't even exist, as their father hadn't seen their mother for over seven years. Michael to young too understand any of this, waited with the others excitedly for his father to arrive.

Around seven that night, the front door slammed open, and a large heavy built man with short black hair appeared. Michael knowing it was his dad ran to him, wanting to be the first to greet him. A backhander sent him flying backwards.

"Where'd this bastard come from?" His father exploded, as his older brothers disappeared back into their rooms. Someone in jail had told his father of his third son's birth several years ago, he had waited patiently for this moment.

"I was raped!" His wife whimpered, as he slapped her to the floor, dragging her by the hair into the lounge room. Kicks and slaps rained down on both Michael and his mother, till his father, tired from the workout, leaned back against the wall. Expecting another beating at any moment, Michael and his mum cowered on the floor crying, too scared to move.

For several minutes, his father stood glaring down at them, breathing heavily. Michael, not understanding, but knowing somehow it was his fault, soiled himself with fear, sobbing uncontrollably in his mother's arms. The standoff continued for what felt like a lifetime, when his father smirking, sat down.

"I'll give you the benefit of the doubt you slut, but this bastard doesn't sleep under my roof. Get him out of here!" His father spat out, as his mother swiftly carried him out the back, to an old tool shed. That night as his father slept, Michael's mother brought out his small bed and what clothing he possessed. He realised from now on that this would be his home, as long as his father lived here.

The shed to Michael had become his prison as if his father's freedom had been exchanged for his incarceration. Ice cold in winter and an oven in summer, he spent most of his miserable childhood a captive of his birth. Somehow he survived his enforced solitude, though it would haunt him for the rest of his life. Even his mother who had nurtured him, calling him her beautiful boy, changed. He became the reason for her maltreatment by her husband, the source of all her troubles.

Meals became irregular and unlike at first, where she brought them out to him, now they were left at the back door. Many times his father in a foul mood or drunk, knocked them over leaving Michael with the option of going hungry or scrapping what he could off the steps. His brothers at first bashed him, trying to curry favour with their father. Even six years their junior, he learnt quickly to defend himself making them back off.

Like many deprived children, stealing to Michael became second nature. He taught himself how to survive, taking what he needed. He became known as a person to avoid. Through all this, he on occasion would sneak to the house window at night and watch his father play with his brothers. He'd stand silently praying for his father would someday forgive him, while the cold penetrated his clothing, making him shiver uncontrollably. At first, he tried to gain his father's love, doing anything he thought might impress him. After several beatings, he learnt it was hopeless, so he just kept away from him.

School became his only escape. Leaving early, coming back late, it gave him an outlet, a needed release from his enforced imprisonment. Here he met and confided in his three friends, getting something from them he lacked at home, love. As the years flowed by, his life became a cycle of abuse and soul-destroying loneliness. His friends became his lifeline, his only link to affection. Without their love, he knew he wouldn't have survived.

One night around 9, while Michael lay shivering, trying to keep warm, he heard the rear door of his family's home fly open. The door banged loudly against the sidewall, as his father stumbled down the three small steps into the backyard. Fearing another beating from his drunken father, Michael whimpering with fear, tried to conceal himself. Throwing himself onto the floor he swiftly crawled under his bed, doing his best to hide.

As the seconds past and nothing occurred, Michael summoning his courage, crawled along the shed floor to a spot where he could see what was going on. Through a crack in the wall, he watched his father grab a shovel from his mother's veggie garden, before swiftly digging a hole. Looking around making sure no one was watching, he placed a large bag in the hole, before filling it in. He then covered the area with some of his mother's pot plants, making sure the area looked untouched.

Without warning, he swiftly turned. Laughing insanely, he tossed his shovel at Michael's shed. At first, Michael feared he'd seen him, cringing back waiting to be belted or worse. Time seemed to drag slowly by as he waited in the dark for the shed door to fly open and the flogging to start. As the seconds crawled by and his father didn't appear, Michael slowly relaxed. Relieved, he assumed that his father was just his usual vindictive self, just trying to scare him. Going back to the crack, he watched his father urinate against his shed and his dinner plate, before retreating back inside, chuckling insanely.

Just after midnight, shouts erupted from the house, as the police arrived. His father and brothers must have put up quite a struggle as smashing and breaking of furniture could be heard clearly from the shed. After things had settled down, the police could be heard searching the house, much to the annoyance of his mother.

"There's nothing here!" She shouted over and over again until she too was dragged away. After the police finished in the house, they started searching outside in the yard. It became clear to Michael that they were looking for what his father had buried earlier. Afterwards, he found out that his dad had gone back to his old trade of robbing banks. Like before he'd been stupid enough to be seen and this time he wouldn't be coming home for 12 years.

During the search, Michael was found by the police in the shed. Outraged by the way he was being treated Community Services was called. Taking him away, they placed him in emergency accommodation, until something could be worked out. His mother several months later was allowed to take him home, where he now lived in the house with his brothers. Regrettably, the damage had been done; Michael no longer regarded them as his family, just somewhere to stay.

One day when his mother and brothers went off to visit his father in jail, Michael secretly dug up what his father had buried. Opening the bag, he found a shotgun plus ten cartridges. The rest of the bag contained tightly rolled bundles of black plastic. Opening one he found a huge amount of money. Michael sat looking at the money for some time, before rewrapping everything. His father must have been stockpiling his money from all his robberies, only using a small amount to live on.

The remainder was here, kept hidden until a time when he could retire and live like a king. Smiling, Michael carried it into his old accommodation in the shed. Here he pulled up some loose timber planks, stowing the bag there, before replacing the boards. Apparently, his mother didn't know of the money, or she would have dug it up herself he concluded. This was his moving away from home money he chuckled, thinking of his father's reaction when he returned to find it gone.

For the next three years, Michael stayed at home, biding his time until he turned 15. Feeling the time was right he left, not even telling his mother, taking what little he owned. Drifting around the area, he lived on the streets, camping out under a bridge over the river. He worked as a carpenter and a brickie's labourer, never really liking the fixed work hour weeks. Taking a job on a farm, he found he had a gift for growing vegetables and fruit. Deciding to someday have his own farm, Michael devised a plan for his future.

During this time, he became involved in the movement to stop the clearing of the native forest. His history of being aggressive and antisocial made him popular at demonstrations. It also made him a target of the local police. Several times he was arrested during these demonstrations and severely beaten. This cause, however, proved his salvation. With his help, the anti-logging movement achieved something positive, when the government caved in, making the area a National Park.

For a while he became a local hero to the alternative lifestyle movement, giving him an outlet to associate with people, other than his three friends. At 17 he secretly returned to his old home retrieving the bag from under the floorboards. Several months later a miracle occurred when Michael had a big win at the racetrack. With the money, he bought a small farm property just outside of the town limits.

There he lived quietly, growing organic vegetables and fruit, making a modest living. What amazed people at the time, was no one could remember where exactly or which race had paid such a huge prize. Despite the doubts the local people and the cops had, Michael paid his taxes on the money he'd won and as far as the law was concerned he was clean.

Jed tripping in front of him brought Michael back to the present. Steadying Jed, Michael decided to watch him more closely as they continued on.

KIRRA

Kirra watched Michael help Jed, and her heart went out to them. She loved them both, they were the closest things to family she had ever had. Unlike Michael, Kirra had grown up in luxury. Her mother's family was wealthy, and her father ran a local company for her mother's brother. Tom, her uncle, was one of the richest men in the country, owning several businesses in the area. Her mother had been a model and quite a catch for her father, who had been a famous footballer. When Kirra was born, she was the oldest of three sisters and by far the prettiest.

As she grew into her teens, unlike her sisters, she rebelled against the beauty pageants her mother insisted she enter. Her two sisters couldn't understand her resentment, loving the contests, which they usually won. Kirra didn't like it one bit, comparing it to being paraded around like a prize cow. At school, as she grew older, the boys flocked to her, asking her out. Sadly they wanted more than she was prepared to give.

From these young men, she found safety by hanging out with Michael and Jed. They listened to her when she told them of her problems, which to them seemed minor compared to their own situations. Through all this, though they still supported her, realising she needed protection from her more aggressive suitors.

On one of her father's many business trips away with the firm, her Uncle Tom volunteered to look after the three girls. Kirra had become aware of her uncle's interest in her, as she approached 17. At first, she'd been appreciative that he spent so much time helping her with her homework and career choices. As time passed her uncle's, indiscreet touching had started to put her on edge. While Kirra was showering upstairs, her uncle's had given her two younger girls a large amount of money to fetch some treats from the local shopping centre. The girls excited at spending so much, left, promising to be back in two hours.

"Take your time I've got work to keep me busy" their uncle laughed, as the two hurried off. Watching the girls disappears down the road, Tom smiling, moved upstairs to Kirra's bedroom. Finding the door unlocked, he entered taking off his clothes. The first warning Kirra had of his presence was the shower curtain being opened behind her. Too shocked to yell, Kirra covered herself looking at her uncle as he stood naked and fully aroused.

"You're going to enjoy this Kirra, as much as me!" Tom sniggered, his eyes locked on her body feasting on it. Moving towards her, he lifted her out of the shower, turning her away from him, trapping her against him. With one hand he reached down between her legs rubbing her sex, while his other hand cupped her right breast, squeezing it painfully. Revolted and in shock, Kirra sobbed in horror as her uncle thrust his organ against her buttocks his excitement making it tremble.

Breathing heavily, her uncle dragged her towards her bed, his hands roaming over her body as he tried to excite her. Pushing her back onto the bed, he fell on top of her trying to kiss her, while his hands pinned her arms beside her head. On top of her now, he smiled down at her as he used his knees to spread her legs.

"Get ready here it comes." He laughed, as he thrust forward, seeking entry. Squirming beneath him Kirra hysterically resisted. Turning her body from side to side her fear turn to anger.

"Get off me!" She screamed out, as a sense of feeling dirty overwhelmed her. Fighting back, she kicked out striking him between the legs, bending him over in agony.

"You fucking bitch!" Tom groaned, sliding from the bed. Paralysed, knowing she would run, he tried to master the pain and capture her again. Seeing her chance, Kirra leapt from the bed. Grabbing the clothes she'd laid out before going in for a shower, she rushed past her uncle. In desperation to stop her, Tom grabbed her legs, tripping her. Luckily, his hands failed to grip her wet skin, allowing her to escape. Free, Kirra ran screaming out into the night, naked and terrified.

Dressing swiftly, sobbing with fear, she hid in the bushes across from her house as her uncle, still in pain, searched for her. Petrified she remained in hiding, fearing for her sisters. When her parents arrived home, she ran to them, only to be slapped by her mother.

"You dirty little tramp!" she shouted, paralysing Kirra. Tom had rung her parents, telling them how their daughter had asked for money for sex. She threatened to say he touched her if he said anything.

"You can't believe that Mum!" Kirra cried as her uncle walked from the house accompanied by her two sisters. Her father seemed torn as he stood there; Kirra saw that he believed her. Then again Tom was his boss, and there was no proof either way, as to what had happened.

"Let's all go inside. We'll speak of it later." Her father suggested. Kirra heartbroken walked dejectedly back into the house.

Halfway up the stairs, Kirra heard her mother apologising to her brother. She promised him she would be punished for her behaviour. Confined to the house as punishment, Kirra's mother would hear nothing more on the subject. Instead, she praised her brother for his morals in refusing her advances. Her two sisters, solidly on their uncle's side, refused to talk to her, totally ignoring her.

Two months after the incident, Kirra arrived home from school to find her sisters and mother had gone out shopping. A note left on the fridge told her to make her own dinner, as her father would be home late as well. Changing out of her school uniform she locked her door, before stepping into the shower. Finished, she walked into her bedroom in her bra and underwear, to find her uncle sitting on her bed, waiting. Screaming this time, she rushed to the door to find the key gone.

"Next time check under your bed before locking the door." He chuckled. Standing he walked towards Kirra, who like a cornered animal, tried to move away from him.

"This time there'll be no escape!" He smiled, as rushing forward he grabbed her hair, dragging her back to the bed. At first, she fought him, trying desperately to keep her underclothes on. Constant slaps and punches to her face and body, took the fight out of her, as Tom ripped her bra and pants from her bruised body. Lying on the bed sobbing, Kirra begged him to leave her alone, as laughing he took off his clothes.

"Next time, don't fight so hard, you'll enjoy it more!" He chuckled, as he prepared to climb on the bed. Using what energy she had left, she tried to kick him as she had before, this time he was ready. Slapping her leg away, he snarled down at her, threatening to kill her if she tried that again. Staring at her his eyes daring her to try again, he grabbed her legs, slowly pulling them apart.

Climbing between them, he positioned himself, starting to enter her. Crying, Kirra looked up seeing her Uncle staring down at her, saliva ran from the corner of his mouth as if he was daring her to try something.

"Are you ready bitch?" He snarled, as his organ began to push deeper. Too scared to do anything, Kirra looked up at her uncle to see him suddenly freeze. Looking at him she saw the tip of a long carving knife burst out of his stomach above her. Her uncle screaming in absolute agony fell sideways off her onto the floor. Groaning loudly, he suddenly stiffened, before going silent.

Standing where her uncle had stood, Kirra saw her father crying.

"I'm so sorry Kirra. I should have done something sooner!" Her father sobbed, covering his daughter's body with a blanket. Carrying her downstairs, he called the police, before driving her to the hospital. Through the whole ordeal at the hospital from the doctor's treatment of her, to the police interviews, Kirra's father stayed with her supporting her. Full of remorse her father told the police what had happened, ashamed of himself, for not doing something sooner.

To Kirra's surprise, her father was arrested and taken to the Police station, leaving her alone at the hospital. Her Uncle Tom's family had powerful friends, who blamed Kirra for the whole affair. Even Kirra's mother backed her family against her husband. Kirra's father once released on bail, tried to convince his wife of her brother's guilt. She would have none of it, ordering him to leave, wanting a divorce.

Heartbroken by his wife's betrayal of him, her father completely broke down, killing himself. Her mother saw his suicide as an admission of guilt, moving home to her family. By the time Kirra left hospital her mother and sisters had moved back to her family's home abandoning her.

Arriving at an empty home, Kirra found a note telling her to get out. Heartbroken she packed her belongings into two bags and left. Four hours of wandering the streets aimlessly, Kirra realised she had only three friends she could turn too. Bella was still living with her family leaving Kirra, only one choice. Grabbing a taxi using what money she had, Kirra went to Michael's farm. Walking the last kilometre when her money ran out, Kirra near breaking point, reached the door wondering what reception she would get.

Knocking on the door, sobbing from shame and humiliation, she was warmly welcomed by her friends. It was two in the morning when she arrived, yet they sat with her for the rest of the night, listening to her story, providing two shoulders to cry on. She never saw her family again, hearing from friends that they had moved north into Queensland. Kirra at first missed them and tried to contact them several times.

In the end, she reached her mother, only to be treated like trash by her. She still blamed her for everything, telling her bluntly not to ring again, before hanging up on her. Devastated by her treatment, Kirra for days was unable to leave her room. Her friends had comforted her, giving her their love letting her know, they were there for her. Kirra had stayed at the farm ever since, knowing that from that day, Jed, Michael and Bella were her only family.

A squeeze of her hand made her look across at Bella, who winked back at her smiling. They were like twins now, sensing each other's thoughts, as Kirra brightened, forgetting the past.

JED

Jed struggled on, behind them, his strength fading fast. Without attracting attention, he dropped another bunch of pills in his mouth. They were killing him, but today was a special day. He wanted to remember this day, as a day they all lived life to the full, and that meant taking pills. Instantly the drug took effect, not lifting him, but reviving him, keeping him going and for today that was good enough.

Jed's family had been a sporting family, addicted to winning. From an early age Jed and his older brother James, ran every morning around the local oval, building up their fitness. Their father was obsessed with his boys being football stars, pushing them hard. While their friends went about being young, Jed and James worked out pushed continuously by their father to be the best. James was bigger, stronger and faster than Jed.

When they practised off field, Jed found James could run rings round him without breaking into a sweat. On field though, James lacked the killer instinct that Jed possessed when dealing out punishment to the opposing teams. No matter how he tried, James always seemed to miss out on the representative school teams, while Jed was always chosen. James wasn't bitter; he loved his brother and applauded his accomplishments on the field. The problem was he just didn't like the brutal element of playing Rugby. James was not an aggressive person. James was gay.

When James first told Jed, he'd been shocked, just standing there frozen. Recovering quickly, he hugged his brother assuring him he still loved him. James overjoyed with Jed's acceptance of him and sensing it was time, went to his parents telling them as well. The reaction this time was far different.

Their father and mother at first were silent looking at each other, as if somehow it was the other parent's fault. Their father then went crazy, changing from outright rage to crying uncontrollably, while their mother sobbed. Cursing James for bringing this evil into their home, their father struck James, knocking him to the floor. Furious, he ordered him to leave the house and not come back. Jed standing up for his brother left as well.

As they both stood outside in the street, James pleaded with Jed to return. He told him that it would all blow over and Jed needed to finish his schooling. Jed heartbroken reluctantly returned, keeping in contact with his brother against his parents' wishes. They met when possible in town, where James now worked employed in the local newspaper as a photographer.

James to Jed seemed happy living on his own, though his parent's rejection of him hurt him deeply. He always talked about how in time they'd welcome him back, forgiving him and accepting his sexuality. A year later he'd contracted AIDS and knowing reconciliation with his family was not going to happen, James in despair, hung himself. That day, Jed's world fell apart.

He gave up rugby and started using. As his life spun out of control, he too was thrown out of home. Sleeping on the street, his addiction became his only reason to live. Hooked, unable to feed his habit, he turned into a waif-like creature, stealing or prostituting himself to raise money. Arrested several times for trafficking and using, Jed, in the end, was sent to jail.

His life became a nightmare of rape and withdrawal, spending most of his time in the prison hospital. Not being a relative, it took Michael weeks to find out where he was being held. When he finally located him, he visited when possible, bringing him both love and hope. The girls tried many times to visit him as well. Jed ashamed wouldn't let them see him, only Michael.

When six months later he was released, Michael and the girls were waiting for him. Weak and near death, Michael took him back to his newly purchased farm, nursing him back to health. Jed could never thank him enough for looking after him practically bringing him back from near death. Michael even supplied him money, to buy just enough drugs to stabilise him. They both knew that it was only putting off the inevitable unless he gave them up. Jed knew deep down that he couldn't.

Several times he did try to kick his addiction, but he'd been using for too long. Coming down to get clean, going cold turkey, just about killed him each time. In the end he only managed to reduce the amount he used, maintaining an air of normality. His condition ate at his very soul, devouring him alive, the only thing that kept him going at all, was the love of his friends. Yet looking back, through all the pain he suffered, through all the heartbreak, it was nothing compared to what happened to Bella, he acknowledged. She walked beside him now, always there, looking after him, as if he was a bird with a broken wing.

BELLA

Of the four, Bella's life had been boringly normal. Raised in a Christian home, she'd enjoyed the love of her family. Going to church every Sunday, she'd learnt there was good in everyone that they all could be saved. That was why she'd bonded with the other three; she could see the goodness in them. Her parents were far from impressed with her choice of friends, warning her to stay away from the three. Bella, in turn, reminded them of the scriptures, silencing their argument.

Although they continued to have their doubts about the three, they left her to make her own decisions and prayed for her. The problem was, as Bella grew older, her time with her friends grew as well. It finally reached a point where she was with them more than her family. Aged seventeen, Bella's parents had given her an ultimatum. Either break off seeing her three friends or move out. Bella had been heartbroken, unable to decide.

In the end, knowing she couldn't live without her friends, she sadly left home, even though she knew the door was always open if she wished to return. Kirra had only been living at the farmhouse for four months when Bella moved in. Kirra and Bella had been close, now they became like sisters. Bella's constant support helped Kirra to come to grips with what had happened to her, letting her move on.

On Michael's eighteenth birthday, Bella reached another crossroad. Going against her beliefs; she lost her virginity to Michael, while Kirra at the same time, made love for the first time, with Jed. They'd all been sitting on the veranda, Bella playing her violin, celebrating Michael's birthday. It was just one of those perfect nights the four shared when Jed pulled Kirra to him kissing her passionately.

They'd all kissed before, many times, but this was somehow different. It was as if the kiss released a hunger in Kirra, freeing her from the ugliness of the attack on her by her uncle. Bella gripped by her feelings for her friends, was overcome by her own hunger, kissing Michael. Knowing she shouldn't, she made no protest as Michael began exploring her body, while over his shoulder she watched Kirra and Jed strip. It became contagious as she too shed her clothing, marvelling at her friend's nakedness.

Undressed, the two couples laughing, changed partner's, continuing their foreplay. Why they'd changed none of them knew, as they fervently explored their new partner's body. Stopping again, the two couples looking at each other, smiling at the situation, swapped back to their original partners. The two boys sensing what was going to happen reluctantly broke away from the girls.

Running inside the house, they dragged two large mattresses out onto the veranda. Throwing them on the floor the girls gathered pillows and blankets, throwing them on top, making a giant bed. All of them then climbed on and began to kiss again, this time more urgent, more passionate, as arousal reached boiling point.

Each couple made love beside the other, the girls crying out as they both lost their virginity together. The veranda became a frenzied movement of limbs, as each couple screamed and moaned their wanton need for satisfaction all-consuming. Resting sated, the girls looked at each other giggling, before swapping, as they became the aggressors. There were no boundaries that night as they swapped back and fourth; trying as many different positions as possible, until exhausted they collapsed sleeping.

They'd made love together many times since then, but always with the same partner, not swapping. They thought of that night, as something symbolic, like a marriage ceremony, between the four of them. It bound them together into an unbreakable union, cementing their strange relationship into normalcy.

For the next year, they lived on the farm, keeping mostly to themselves. They scraped out an existence by growing organic vegetables and fruit, selling them at the local markets. Their lives although simplistic, were full of fun and love as their relationship grew. Other alternative groups that flourished on the North Coast found the four odd to say the least. Mind you, they mostly kept to themselves, keeping out of trouble and to the locals that was all that mattered.

Turning nineteen, Bella's life changed forever, as she prepared to enter University. It had always been her dream to play in an orchestra. Jed's insistence that she see it through paid off. After a two-year break from school, she had applied for a grant to study music at the local University. After completing an arduous entry exam, she was amazed when she finished in the top five. She'd been so excited, squealing with joy when the letter of acceptance had arrived.

Then came the pivotal moment, when at the peak of her University studies, she was asked to do a recital. She could still see the jealous looks on the other student's faces when it was announced during their lecture that she had been chosen. Remembering that time again, her eyes slowly filled with tears.

"I won't ruin today by thinking of that." She said out loud, wiping her eyes, as Kirra next to her, squeezed her hand comforting her.

"We're nearly there!" Jed screamed startling them all, as he saw the warning sign that marked the deep waterhole. Hurrying forward, the four friends laughed and shouted, listening to their echoes return back to them from the surrounding hills. Stripping off their clothes, plunging into the deep cold water, they forgot their cares, letting the water drown their worries.

Floating in the Billabong, an uneasy peace settled over the four as they each contemplated the paths their lives had taken to reach this point. Floating on their backs, their mouths just clear of the water and their ears submerged, the only sounds they heard was the odd splash as someone's foot broke the surface.

"Is this how you feel after death?" Bella asked herself, as the soundless roar of her indecision pounded inside her head. Shaking herself, she swam to the bank. Resting on her back in the shallows her eyes closed, she felt the others join her. They lay there enjoying the water's chilly embrace, recovering from their early morning walk. Once their bodies had cooled, the four walked out of the water, lying down on a grass-covered area, around an old campfire. Closing their eyes they rested, letting the sun warm their naked bodies.

Twenty minutes of rest found Kirra and Bella dry and replenished. Winking at each other, they straddled the man opposite, kissing him. The two women smiled at each other, as they seductively used their hands and mouths to excite their partners. Overwhelmed, with both watching and participating, the four were driven into a frenzy of stimulation waking an uncontrollable hunger.

Their lovemaking became intense, as each couple once sated, swapped partners starting again, as they had the first time, so long ago. Everything else in life became irrelevant, as they became overwhelmed by the moment, making love countless times with both their partners, screaming with joy, pushing each of their partners to the limit. Finished, too tired to talk, they'd slept, each remembering why they were here and how it had begun.

BELLA THE SAINT
AUTUMN 2000

Bella's excitement was infectious, as she danced with her friends, eager for the night ahead. Tonight she would perform for the Dean of the University, Professor Davison and his close friend Doctor Clark. Clark was a well-known and gifted surgeon, heading up the surgical treatment section of the local hospital. Several times during the year, the Dean asked the most promising musical students to do a recital at his residence.

It was an incredible honour for Bella, being the first picked this year. Success at these private concerts promised a bright future for the students chosen. Bella's friends were sure she would shine, having seen her dedication to her music. Her parents too were overjoyed, although it was for another reason. They hoped her success, would encourage Bella to break away from her strange friends. They knew that to follow her career, she would have to leave the farm and seductive brainwashing; they feared her three perverted friends held her under.

Jed was overjoyed at Bella being selected, having reintroduced her, to her passion for playing. He had been the one who'd bought the violin for her, after hearing her play it in a second-hand shop. Money at the time was short, so Jed had gone without, to scrape together enough to purchase it for her. He would remember that moment forever; seeing her both laugh with happiness, then cry with joy, knowing what it meant to him to get it for her. It had been one of those rare moments in his life when he'd given something in the name of love and been richly rewarded.

The night of the Recital, her three friends had thrown together a special dinner for her, to show how proud they were of her. She laughed uncontrollably, putting off leaving until the last minute. When the time came for her to leave, they'd all gathered outside, wishing her luck as she'd cycled away. Michael at first had wanted to drive her, but fuel was short, so she opted to ride her bike. It was just over twenty minutes travelling time through the Lismore Township, to the Dean's house. Michael's farm was just south of the town, while the Dean's house was on the northern side, so to be careful she allowed an hour.

Bella rode merrily along happy with life, hoping tonight was a success. She knew that a career in music would not only help her but would also help her friends. Times had been hard for them, and she hoped with some extra money to help make all their lives easier. It was a beautiful starlit night, as she joyfully pedalled along the road, taking her time, in no real hurry. Reaching the outskirts of the town, she increased speed past an abandoned old warehouse. She knew it was silly, but a week ago she'd seen the outline of a man in the shadows watching her.

Whoever it was, had been standing beside an old warehouse, as she pedalled by on her way home. It was just getting dark, and she'd been momentarily frightened, by the silent shadow. Overcoming her fear she'd called out "hello" to the shadow, receiving no answer. There was something about the way the person continued to stand there unmoving and not replying, which made her apprehensive. She was just about to repeat her hello, when a passing car made her concentrate on her steering, before turning back. The shadow she seen had now disappeared.

Continuing on towards home, she spent the next ten minutes watching the road behind her. For some reason, she sensed he meant to hurt her, expecting him at any moment to appear behind her, coming after her. He hadn't and later she had laughed about it with her friends, putting it down to a case of nerves. Still, for some reason every time she passed through this area, she was wary.

Entering the town itself, she passed an old sandstone church, run now by an ex-biker who'd found God. Spotting the priest, Bella shouted his name, waving merrily. Ben, the priest, returned the wave, always happy to see Bella.

"Where are you off to young lady?" Ben shouted out, wondering where she was heading. The priest knew her well, as she occasionally dropped in to talk about religion or her friends. She lived on the south side and her parents the west, so where was she going he mused? Not hearing him clearly, she waved again, pedalling towards the bridge, crossing the river onto the north side of town.

"Well, it's none of my business," Ben said to himself smiling, as he waited for his congregation to arrive. Still, Bella filled his mind long after she'd disappeared from view. She was a girl in an emotional minefield. On the one hand, she had her Christian upbringing, something she genuinely believed in. On the other hand, she was in a relationship with three other people. She'd confessed to him about her sleeping with both men, sharing them with Kirra. She also admitted being deeply in love with Kirra, although the women themselves didn't sleep together.

She'd told him also of their ritual marriage where she'd lost her virginity, making love with both men at the same time along with Kirra. She felt that it was different but okay by God's teachings, as they loved each other. She wanted his opinion. At first, he'd been speechless having never dealt with this type of sin before. And that's what the church called it, a sin. He had his doubts.

Love shone out of Bella when she talked about her relationships with her partners. She had pointed out, that many men had more than one wife in the old days in the Bible, so why couldn't she love two men? Ben had met Kirra, Jed and Michael, finding them all caring and loving people. He also sensed that they all had emotional scars from their separate pasts, which worried him. He theorised that this may have somehow affected their mental stability, causing this unusual sexual arrangement, though he couldn't be sure. This semi-married state they were in, questioned his own reasoning, as he found they had bonded together like man and wife.

In the end, he told her to pray about it, telling her he could not judge her for her love. He knew he'd taken the coward's way out, wanting to keep seeing her. He knew that if he peddled the church line, that sin was sin and she must repent, she'd turn her back on the church and him. It came down to the fact that he liked her and didn't want her abandoning her faith or his friendship.

Peddling faster turning left over the concrete bridge that marked the end of the city centre, Bella rode to the entrance of the Dean's farm. Dean Davison and Doctor Clark lived together on a ten-acre property, the house located on a small hilltop, which overlooked the township. Riding her bike to the front gate, Bella decided to hide it, rather than have someone passing by take it. Walking it along the property boundary, she leaned it up against a side hedge hoping no one would see it there.

The Dean's garage was located around the back of his house, so she figured leaving it here, was better than turning up at the back door. Removing her violin from the bike rack, she checked her clothing. Satisfied that she looked presentable, she walked up to the front entrance, her heart pounding.

"This is it." She whispered. "Tonight will change all of our lives forever," Bella told herself smiling, as she knocked on the front door. She didn't know how true those words would be.

The Recital

Dean Davison and Dr Clark were two of the most eligible bachelors on the North coast. Both men had been married, though now they were both divorced. They lived together, on this property owned by the Dean. Many women had tried to land these two big fish, but no one had succeeded yet. 'Too married to their work' most people thought, knowing their demanding work schedules, kept them away from the local nightlife. Bella was the first student this year to perform for them, and as she knocked on the door, her nerves started making her shake.

The door opened seconds later, and Dean Davison made her welcome. He told her he'd listened to her music many times at the University over the last few weeks and had been more than impressed. Relieved, her tension flowed away, as he led her into the lounge area. Telling her that Clark had to finish a few reports before joining them, he asked her merrily to limber up, before he arrived.

She quickly went through several pieces she'd practised, getting a feel for her instrument, tuning it up slightly refining the sound it produced. The Dean, watching her perform seemed impressed giving a hearty clap or a smile of approval after each piece was played.

"Where is that doctor, he's missing everything," Davison said smiling, as he went to the door yelling out to Clark. "You have a break and drink something. I'll see where he's got to." The Dean suggested appearing none too happy with his friend's no show. Once he'd left, Bella thirsty, walked to a side table containing several different juices and some fruit. Pouring herself a large glass of orange juice she drank it swiftly, before sitting down on the lounge to wait.

Several minutes passed, and no one had appeared, so she decided to play one of her signature pieces. These were her favourites, the ones she enjoyed playing and the ones she excelled at. She hoped while the two men weren't there, to get these ones down pat before playing it again when the Dean and Clark appeared. She began strongly, working her way through the first section, the violin practically singing. During the middle section she began to feel sleepy, missing some important notes.

Stopping, upset by her lack of concentration, she stretched her arms trying to bring herself back into focus. Instead, she became drowsy her legs failing her as she collapsed back onto the lounge. Knowing something was wrong, she tried to sit up as she tumbled sideways, landing on the floor. Through bleary eyes, terror gripped her, as she saw a pair of naked feet standing over her. Looking up through bleary eyes she saw the Dean standing above her completely nude.

"It's too soon!" She heard a voice behind him yell out, as she fought to move, finding her limbs only partially responded.

"I'm not waiting a second longer!" the Dean growled. Reaching down, he manhandled Bella back onto the lounge. Laying her down, he grabbed her clothing. Ripping her dress down the front; he tore it from her body. Clark behind him, forgetting his caution, came forward, cutting off her underwear with a small sharp knife.

"Help me!' Bella tried to scream, only to hear a faint croak instead.

"Oh, we're going to help you alright. Once we're finished with you, you'll be a new person." Davison chuckled, thrusting his hand between Bella's legs, making her moan in agony.

"Yes you won't know yourself and remember less, but you'll feel everything." Clark laughed, shoving a needle into Bella's arm, as she silently wept, praying for someone to save her. Grabbing a leg each, the two men dragged her limp body down the hallway. In a futile effort to save herself, Bella grabbed hold of the railing of the staircase leading upstairs.

"She's a strong one isn't she?" Clark smiled, kicking her in the stomach, breaking her flimsy hold on the railing.

"Yes, it's going to be quite a night," Davison admitted chuckling, as he pressed the hidden button to their secret playroom in the basement. Dragging Bella down the stairs, they manhandled her onto a specially built giant bed, in the middle of the room. Davison then tied her hands to the bedpost, as Clark unable to wait a moment longer, jumped on top of her.

Entering her roughly he repeatedly bit her flesh, slapping her repeatedly. As she groaned in pain, Clark giggled insanely, enjoying the sound of her misery. Davison drooling, watched like a rabid dog, as Clark viciously continued his assault. Bella, her emotional stability destroyed, shut down as her mind tried to protect her from her physical abuse.

Clark uncaring kept thrusting into her, not even noticing her silence. Screaming in pleasure Clark came, as Davison remotely controlled a camera above the bed, set up for their special nights. Both men took turns raping her, as each man tried to punish her for something in their dark past, which made them hate all women. Grabbing a small whip, Davison then beat her, covering her body with welts and cuts. Aroused by the beating, each man again took his turn raping and sodomising her, as the other looked on, screaming encouragement.

Above them, the camera unemotionally kept filming, recording her every humiliation for their future entertainment. Time seemed to slow for Bella, as each man inflicted whatever perverted punishment he could think of, to break her. Relentlessly they beat her trying to make her scream to satisfy their hunger for her sufferance. In the end, tired of beating their plaything, they both rested.

"God, this plaything was the best night yet!" Clark screamed hysterically, as Davison giggling beside him, looked down admiring their handy work.

"Too bad she stopped screaming. It somehow wasn't as much fun." Davison pointed out.

"I thought it was good in a way, makes her special somehow. Problem is we went a bit far." Clark smiled, Davison begrudgingly agreeing.

"Yes, there will be no visiting her later I'm afraid."

"What do you suggest?"

"Dump her on the other side of town, I know just the spot." Looking down Clark observed Bella starting to move as their drug cocktail started to wear off.

"Looks like she's still got some energy yet. I'll just give her another lesson." He grinned pulling her roughly into the middle of the bed.

"You never fail to amaze me, Doctor." Davison laughed watching his friend.

Finished with her, they drove the blood covered remains of their night's entertainment to the local tip. Tossing her on the ground beside the front gate, they then covered her with garbage, before driving off.

"Should've killed her." The Dean pointed out, as they drove home. Unlike Clark he thought leaving them alive was risky.

"She won't last the night. Anyway, we agreed there'd no killing at home. It's too hard to get the blood out of the carpet as it is!" Doctor Clark sniggered, making Davison chuckle.

"I've got a couple of operations tomorrow morning and need some sleep, will you be able to tidy up?" Clark asked neutrally.

"No problem my friend, I'll take care of it. And anyway, someone might call looking for our plaything, can't have them suspicious can we." Davison replied, tomorrow being his rostered day off, he'd be at home anyway.

"Do you think we'll have any trouble with this one?" Clark asked.

"No, I checked her out. She's just a druggie slut living with a couple of deadbeats. No one will care less about her death. And even if we do have trouble, it should be easy to point the blame at someone else" Davison smiled.

"That's what I like about you my friend; you have an answer for every scenario." Clark sniggered, as they hurried home to shower.

Morning

That next morning at 4:00am, the first garbage truck pulled up next to the gates. Their job was to clean away the rubbish dumped the night before by people not wanting to pay the tip fees. George, the passenger, hopped out of the truck preparing to clean the mess up, as Joe the driver, reversed into position to pick up the rubbish. Going through the pile, George scooped up shovel after shovel, throwing them casually into the rear bucket.

It never failed to amaze him how wasteful people could be, as he continued to shovel load after load of household rubbish into the dump bin. Most of the fruit and vegetables he loaded, looked edible, and he knew the high cost of groceries at the moment. Looking down at his shovel as it hit something solid, he saw the end of a leg appear.

At first, he didn't believe his eyes, as with a sense of foreboding he pushed the rubbish to the side. To his horror, he saw the blood covered naked body of a woman. Unable to speak, George felt his body double over in pain, as he emptied his stomach onto the ground next to the body.

Joe the driver looking back, saw George vomit onto the ground. He'd been working with him for over six months, and this was the first time he'd seen him throw up his breakfast. Getting out of the truck, Joe walked to the back of the truck smiling. He was about to make a funny remark about George's weak gut when he saw George was kneeling down on the ground in the garbage.

Thinking he really was crook, he quickly moved forward. Looking down over his workmate's shoulder, he saw the body, backing up in shock.

"Oh my God!" Joe whispered, taking in the full horror of the broken body.

"Call an ambulance Joe. Make it quick, she's still alive!" George choked out, as with tears cascading down his cheeks he covered Bella's body with his jacket.

The Detectives

Detective Dave Johnson laid curled up next to his wife Helen, enjoying every moment of his seventh day off. It had been a hard couple of months and now with the Christmas school holiday break over, he'd been granted a whole week off. The holiday season brought its usual mix of schoolies enjoying their first taste of adulthood and the predators who took full advantage of their naivety. Byron Bay, Lismore and Nimbin formed Australia's golden triangle, awash with drugs and the criminal element that lived off it.

Ice had become the cheap heroin, and in tablet form, it saved the user finding a needle. The dealers this year had been giving it away to the kids, letting them get a taste. After three hits you were hooked, taking your new addiction home with you, a great present for Christmas. This year they'd been ready, hitting the dealers hard, before they had time to get the product out.

It hadn't made them popular with the youth in the area, here for a good time, many upset by the heavy police presence. Johnson personally couldn't give a shit what people thought, he had two teenage daughters himself and getting rid of these parasites was all he cared about. Drugs, stealing and assaults were down this year, thanks to their presence. Only rape was way up.

Most rapes started with drink spiking in local pubs and clubs. It involved slipping something into a girl's drink while she was out on the town. She was then carried outside by a so-called, 'Good Samaritan', who then raped her. Most of these assaults never got to court, as the girl was usually so drunk beforehand, that she couldn't remember anything. These to Johnson were a waste of time; 'chasing phantoms' he called them.

Then there was the other form of rape where the perpetrator waited for their victims, viciously attacking them, leaving them emotionally and physically abused. This type was the one that got Dave and his partner Detective Ross Luke really going. They both hated these monsters that attacked from the dark, inflicting unimaginable horror on their victims. Detective Luke's own daughter, Jenny, had been one of these victims.

Several witnesses had seen her walking from the township of Byron after the New Year's Eve celebrations. One witness, who admitted having drunk too much and had crashed in his car for the night, gave them their best lead. He saw two men in their thirties, in a brown delivery type van, stop behind the missing girl's car. One he said had walked off towards Byron, while the other appeared to be changing the rear tyre in his van for some reason.

After that, he'd blacked out and gone to sleep. It was the only description they had of her abductors.

It had taken a shattered Ross, two years to recover from his daughter's disappearance. Now as Dave's daughters grew older, his mission in life was to put as many of these bastards behind bars as possible.

His mobile phone ringing beside him brought Johnson out of his sound sleep, back to reality.

"Who the hell is it?" Johnson growled into his phone, knowing whoever was ringing him, better have a good reason for doing it. Sitting up on the side of the bed groggily, he glanced at the clock, seeing it was just approaching five.

"Dave its Ross here. We've got something, bad mate!" Detective Ross Luke informed him, sounding upset.

"Spit it out," Dave replied, coming fully awake. For the next ten minutes, Ross brought him up to speed with the finding of Bella's body. He didn't need a vivid description of what had happened; Dave could tell by Luke's voice how bad it was.

"Pick me up in ten, I'll be waiting," Dave ordered, swiftly dressing, before hurrying downstairs. Back in his bedroom, his wife stared at the ceiling having heard most of the conversation.

"Go get em love and be careful," Helen said softly, before going back to sleep, knowing her husband's hatred of these monsters.

Arriving at the hospital at 6:00 Dave and Ross looked on as the Emergency staffed worked on the bloody, beaten body.

"Fuck what a mess," Dave whispered, seeing the girl's parents sitting in the corner.

"Yeah, I don't think I've seen worse on someone still alive!" Ross replied softly, as Dave walked across to the parents.

"I'm Detective Dave Johnson, and this is Detective Ross Luke, can you tell us anything you know about what happened to Bella?" Dave asked, reading her name from his pad.

"She was going to do a Recital last night. It would've changed her life." Bella's father stammered out, trying to hold it together, as his wife sobbed.

"What recital?" Dave asked.

"For Dean Davison, she'd just entered University and had been honoured by doing a Recital for him at his house. This must've happened instead," he said breaking down and crying.

"Any idea who might be responsible?" Ross asked softly, sharing the man's pain.

"Those two low life's she lives with!" Her father exploded "They wanted to stop her leaving." He cried out, collapsing down next to his wife, unable to continue. Both detectives look at each other, trying to figure out what was going on. In the end, Bella's mother explained.

"Bella's been living on a farm outside of town, a kind of commune. There are two men there, named Michael and Jed. They seem to have some sort of demonic hold over her. She told us that this recital could mean big changes in her life including travelling. We thought the two men mightn't be happy with her leaving." Bella's mum informed them.

"Well, we better go have a talk with these two men. Don't worry, if they're the ones, they'll pay." Dave promised them, as Ross wrote down the address.

Back in their car, the two detectives sat quietly, thinking over the interview with Bella's parents. Checking where the address was on the map, Ross turned to Dave for advice.

"How are we going to handle this?" Ross asked as he started the car.

"We're going in heavy, call for backup, we'll meet them there."

"What about the Dean?" Ross enquired.

"Ring them and see if she was there. I bet she never made it! By the sound of it, these two creeps stopped her on the way I'd say." Dave put forward.

"Sounds like it to me too" Ross concluded, as they drove towards Michael's farm.

The Arrest

Kirra was awoken by a loud bang, as the front door of their home caved in. This was followed by the yelling of 'Police' as police officers stampeded through their farmhouse.

"What's going on?" She yelled as Michael and Jed were dragged from their beds and beaten.

"These two are under arrest for rape." A plainclothes detective informed her, giving her a look as if she was a tramp.

"They've been here all night!" Kirra screamed, getting thrown back against the wall for her trouble.

"Bullshit they have. If I were you, I'd get out of town!" The same detective spat out, as he walked out the door. Michael and Jed, covering their heads from the blows being delivered, were dragged outside and thrown into a police van

"Who are they supposed to have raped!" Kirra screamed after them.

"The other girl who lives here named Bella." The detective said bluntly, before jumping into his car. Kirra stood there in shock before she collapsed onto the ground.

"There's got to be a mistake!" Kirra screamed, regaining her feet.

"There's no mistake. She was found at the tip this morning, barely alive." The Detective informed her angrily, his voice showing he cared about what had happened.

"She left here to go to the Dean's house for a recital at 7 last night. After that, she was going to her parent's home." Kirra cried, wanting the cop to believe her.

"Were you with the two men all night?" the Detective asked.

"Up until 9 then we went to bed in our separate rooms," Kirra answered.

"So they could've left?" the Detective suggested.

"Why would they? They loved Bella." Kirra replied sobbing.

"Maybe they were jealous, that their second slut was leaving, who knows." He answered, before starting his car and leaving Kirra in a cloud of dust. Watching the cops leave, Kirra unsure, returned to the house. Looking around at their broken home, she burst into tears, before dressing and starting the long walk to the hospital.

Lock Up

"Confess you little shit!" Detective Luke screamed, slapping Jed across the head with a closed fist.

"I didn't do anything, especially to Bella." Jed sobbed, trying to come to grips with Bella being hurt.

"She wanted to leave, didn't she? That's why you and your mate pounded her. Didn't you?" Dave Johnson growled, kicking Jed in the shins with his metal-tipped boots, as Jed howled in pain.

"Sarge, take it easy!" Officer Hall yelled from the cell door.

"Piss off Constable! That's an order!" Ross shouted back, as Officer Hall, reluctantly retreated, followed by Johnson.

"Now where was I?" Ross asked himself, before hitting Jed in the kidneys, doubling him up in pain. Officer Hall outside paced the corridor, angry with his superior for dismissing him.

"Let it go, Brett. Ross has lost his daughter to scum like these two" Dave informed him.

"If they did it?" Brett replied angrily.

"If you want to be a detective Brett, you'd better learn to play ball," Dave replied, before leaving Brett to return to the cell with Ross. They'd been at this all day and most of the night, trying to break these two dirtbags. So far they'd had no success. Finished with Jed again, they had Michael brought back in.

"Congratulations Michael! Looks like you'll be joining your dad!" Dave laughed, as Ross slapped him across the shoulder with a nightstick.

The pain was unbelievable as Michael terrified, cowered in his chair, waiting for the next one.

"Why did you do it, Michael? Why did you hurt Bella?" Dave asked softly, watching Michael start to cry.

"I'd never hurt Bella. No matter what anyone says it wasn't me." Michael replied truthfully, receiving another blow.

"Well, we'll soon know my boy. The hospital just rang, she's conscious and talking," Ross informed him, before leaving the cell, locking it behind him.

"When I return, we'll arrange your transport to Grafton jail. The big ugly men there will show you, two pretty boys, a real good time." Johnson laughed, watching Jed shrink back in his cell.

"Yeah, looks like you two will be getting married," Ross added, laughing, as they left.

When Michael, was sure they'd gone, he called out to Jed.

"Are you there Jed?"

"Yeah, Michael I'm here. Is Bella okay?" Jed replied, sobbing.

"I think so. The Detective said they were going to talk to her." Michael replied, wiping the blood from his mouth.

"Why are they doing this to us?" Jed sobbed. "We should be there for Bella."

"I don't know Jed. I guess we're easy targets for them." Michael replied, sounding miserable.

"I'm scared Michael! I can't go back to jail it would kill me." Jed confessed, sounding near breaking point.

"Hang on Jed. They'll find who did it, don't worry." Michael assured him, as the two friends tried to get some rest before their ordeal continued. Sitting in the corner of the cellblock, Officer Hall listened silently.

"If they're guilty, I'm a monkey's uncle," He said to himself angrily, as getting up he raced to his car, driving to the hospital.

THE HOSPITAL

Bella stirred slowly, as the pain of her injuries tried to overwhelm her. Looking at first through blurry eyes, she tried to focus on her surroundings. Shape became discernible, as her parents came into focus.

"Mum" Bella croaked out, as her mother rushed over, kissing her lightly on the cheeks. Standing beside her mum was her dad. He'd been crying she saw, but her father's face showed something else, anger.

"It okay baby, that Michael and Jed will get what's coming to them!" Her father growled.

"What have they got to do with this?" Bella asked not understanding, as her parents looked at each other.

"Those two degenerates at the farm raped you. They then dumped you at the tip, don't you remember?" Her mother asked crying.

"No, I remember playing for the Dean and getting tired. The only other thing I remember is seeing the Dean coming towards me naked." Bella replied softly sounding confused, as her pain started to throb through her entire body.

"Bella, the Dean's a decent man, why would he be naked? You're confused; those troublemakers drugged you and then did this to you before you could leave!" Her father spat out angrily, as a nurse appeared.

"Might be best if you let her rest!" The nurse suggested, as Bella's parents giving the nurse an evil look, reluctantly walked out to the waiting room.

"Thank you, nurse," Bella said softly, pain knifing through her every time she moved. "Is anyone else here?" Bella whispered.

"Yes there's a girl named Kirra, she's been here since yesterday when you were brought in. Your parents wouldn't let her in." the Nurse informed her secretively.

"Can you get her for me?" Bella pleaded. Without a reply, the nurse disappeared into the waiting room. Seeing Kirra sitting quietly in the corner, she approached her.

"Bella said you could come in." The nurse informed her.

"Where's she going nurse? She's not to see our daughter." Bella's father screamed startling everyone in the waiting room.

"Your daughter is over eighteen. She has asked to see her friend. I suggest you keep your voice down." The nurse answered, accompanying Kirra back inside, as Bella's father stood glaring at them both.

The first thing Bella noticed about Kirra, were her red eyes, as she slowly approached her bed. Sobbing, Kirra put her hand in her mouth to stop from screaming, when she saw what Bella looked like. Sitting down beside her, Kirra carefully held Bella's hand, saying nothing, just being there. After several minutes had passed, Bella feeling more confident broke the silence.

"Where are Jed and Michael?" Bella whispered.

"The cops took them! Said they hurt you. Do you know who did this?" Kirra replied, her face a mixture of emotions.

"I'm not sure Kirra. It's all a blur." Bella told her moaning with pain. The nurse hearing her voice adjusted the drip, giving more pain relief, as the two Detectives arrived at the door. Seeing Kirra there they swiftly launched into a series of questions.

"Bella, my name's Detective Johnson, are you sure you don't remember who it was?" Johnson asked from the door, startling Kirra and the nurse, as he and Detective Luke entered the room, moving next to Bella's bed.

"No Detective it's fuzzy. I remember playing for the Dean, then seeing the Dean naked. That's all." Bella answered sounding weak.

"You don't remember Jed and Michael attacking you?" Detective Luke asked bluntly, looking at Kirra.

"There is no way Jed and Michael would hurt me, detective. We're family." Bella smiled weakly, before closing her eyes.

"You're safe here Bella, you can tell us the truth." Detective Johnson growled looking at Kirra accusingly.

"I am telling the truth, I just can't remember!" Bella screamed in pain, as collapsing back onto the pillow she passed out. The nurse seeing what had occurred rushed to Bella's side.

"She's sleeping. She has had one major operation already with another due this afternoon. I will not have her upset again, I suggest everyone leave." The nurse forcefully told them, as the two detectives and Kirra departed. Once in the waiting room, the detectives angrily turned on Kirra.

"You got to her didn't you?" Detective Johnson growled, making Kirra shrink back away from him.

"I did nothing of the sort. You heard what Bella said, she saw the Dean naked. Shouldn't you be asking him some questions?" Kirra replied angrily.

"He's not under suspicion, Jed and Michael are!" Detective Luke replied as Officer Hall entered, standing with Bella's family.

"Why don't you stop interfering and let the police do their job!" Bella's father shouted, surprising everyone with his angry outburst.

"Michael and Jed did nothing!" Kirra shouted back, as Bella's parents stood there glaring at her.

"She was a beautiful innocent girl before she met you, three thugs! Now, look at her! You should be behind bars with your two friends!" Bella's mother cried out, attracting the attention of everyone within hearing distance. Realising they were causing a scene Bella's father grabbed his wife and headed for the door.

"I thought you'd want to know who did this, not who you wanted it to be!" Kirra yelled at them, as Bella's parents ignoring her, left. Collapsing into a seat, Kirra looked down at her hands seeing them shaking uncontrollably

"I could arrest you for hindering an investigation," Johnson growled standing over her threateningly.

"Well go ahead, but you better be right, or I'll get legal aid and sue your arse off." Kirra angrily shouted back, making the two detectives hesitate.

"We'll come back later. Officer Hall, now you're here, you can stay and get statements." Johnson ordered as he and Detective Luke departed.

Walking out to their car, Ross kept thinking about what Bella had said about the Dean. He, like Dave, thought the two druggies were involved, though Bella seemed sure she'd seen the Dean naked.

"Do you think we should do a follow up on what Bella said about the Dean?" Ross asked Dave, as they arrived at their car.

"Yeah, we'll send Hall, he thinks he's the 'Super Detective', let him interview them. Other than that, I'm not dragging two respected men in on the word of some druggie's whore, who thinks she saw a man naked. Shit, I'm amazed she didn't throw in a flying fucking white horse!" Johnson chuckled, as the two detectives drove away.

Once his detective superiors had left, Officer Hall walked over to Kirra, passing her his handkerchief. He was angry with the two senior detectives for not listening. He thought Michael and Jed were dirtbags too, but a crime had been committed, and he wanted the right people caught. Sitting down next to Kirra, Brett got out his pad, getting as many details as possible.

"Why won't they believe me?" Kirra asked crying again when Brett had finished writing.

"It's who you are. Let's face it; none of you are exactly upright citizens." Brett informed her, waiting for her angry reply. None came, as she sat there silently, trying to work out what to do.

"Are the boys okay?" Kirra asked softly, wanting to know.

"They're a bit roughed up, other than that they're okay," Brett replied softly.

"Will they let them go?" Kirra asked.

"Most probably tomorrow, I'd say. Without Bella identifying them, there's no evidence to hold them." Brett told her confidently.

"That's something I suppose," Kirra replied sadly. "Will someone question the Dean?

"That, I can guarantee you." Brett smiled, knowing someone would have to do it after Bella's statement. He wondered how far they could push it though. He knew the Dean and Doctor Clark by reputation, it would be a brave man to push them on the word of a doped up witness.

Taking down anything he thought relevant, Brett left after getting the nurse in charge's name, He decided to come back later to see if anything else came to mind. It would also give him a chance to talk again with the friendly and attractive nurse, he thought smiling.

Inside the emergency department, Bella lay exhausted, after having fought for her life, she now tried desperately to remember. Unfortunately, it was all a blur. All she remembered was playing her violin, better than she'd ever played before, then nothing. Concentrating she saw again the Dean enter the room naked, then a voice saying 'It's too soon'.

'Could they have drugged me?' Bella thought, remembering the juice.

"Feeling better?" The same Nurse asked, holding her hand and applying a cuff to her upper arm, to monitor her blood pressure.

"A little, thank you," Bella replied softly, thinking.

"You had us worried there for a while." The nurse confessed smiling.

"Nurse, do you know Doctor Clark?" Bella watched the nurse hesitate and look towards the door before answering.

"A little, he's the top surgeon here, why?" She answered softly, watching the door.

"I think this was done to me by Professor Davison and Doctor Clark. I don't know why, but it fits." She confessed, watching the nurse. Nurse Black at first couldn't answer, thinking of the ramifications if what she said was true.

"I don't know what to say, Bella. If you're right, they should both go to jail. It's proving it." Nurse Black whispered, before moving off.

"And who's going to believe a druggie whore?" Bella groaned, stopping the nurse dead in her tracks before she resumed walking again. Bella saw in the nurse's eyes that she wasn't convinced that it was Dr Clark and Dean Davison that had attacked her. Who could blame her, when even she had doubts? She tried again to concentrate on what had occurred. Like before her memory became disjointed. Lying in pain, Bella hoped with time that her mind would be clear enough for her to know the truth.

"Thank God, another terrible shift is over!" Nurse Black said to herself, her shift over, she prepared to leave. After her talk with Bella, she'd finished her notes on Bella's condition, before gathering up the scrapings of semen and DNA taken from Bella. Sealing them for transport to the crime lab in Sydney, she dropped them into the Police Evidence safe as she walked out to the locker room and changed. Picking up her gear, she walked back past the evidence locker seeing Doctor Clark standing beside it, with his surgical gloves on.

"Can I help you, doctor?" Nurse Black asked, startling Doctor Clark, who swiftly turned towards her, removing his gloves.

"No, I'm alright, just waiting for a colleague." He volunteered, watching her, as she continued out the door. Thinking of what Bella told her, the nurse feeling a little scared, hurried to her car, wondering if maybe she should tell someone. Then again all she'd seen was him standing next to the evidence box, that wasn't proof of anything she surmised, as she drove off, glad to be going home.

Behind her standing just down from her car, Doctor Clark watched her drive away. Writing down her license plate number and a brief description of her car, he then turned and walked back to the hospital. The nurse he noticed seemed suspicious of him and a little scared, he smiled. She hadn't really seen anything anyway, but he didn't like loose ends, and he knew how to deal with them.

Chuckling to himself he walked down to the basement climbing into his car. Sitting there, he thought again of the nurse. She had a good body; he wondered what it would sound like when she screamed.

Kirra maintained a vigil at the hospital, only leaving briefly to change clothes. Bella's parents returned in the evening, only staying a short time avoiding Kirra. Bella, for the most part, slept, her body closing down, while it tried to repair the damage. The nurses taking pity on Kirra allowed her inside the critical care unit from time to time, where she could sit beside Bella's bed, watching over her. Because this section was restricted, containing the most severely ill patients, she couldn't try to talk to her, all she could do was be there for her.

Someone stroking her hair woke Kirra. Opening her eyes; she found Jed and Michael standing beside her. Hugging them, Kirra seeing Bella was still asleep, led them out to the waiting room.

"God you two look awful." Kirra cried, upset by the treatment the cops had given them.

"Yeah, the bastards really worked us over. Even though, if I were them, I'd do the same to the guys who hurt Bella." Michael admitted angrily.

"She looks so broken." Jed sobbed, as Kirra feeling his pain held him.

"She'll be better when she sees you two," Kirra replied smiling.

"Does she know who did it?" Michael asked.

"She's not sure. The only thing she remembers is seeing the Dean naked, coming towards her." Kirra replied softly, looking around knowing it sounded weird.

"Are the cops going after him?" Jed asked.

"I'm not sure. The young Officer I talked to will I think. The others are convinced it was you two." Kirra replied, seeing the hurt look on their faces. "Hey forget it. The main thing is to make Bella better, so let's get back in there." Kirra smiled, grabbing both their hands and leading them back to Bella's bed.

To Kirra's surprise as they approached the bed she saw Bella's eyes were open, Michael and Jed moved to stand beside the bed reaching out to touch her hand. As if their touch electrocuted her, Bella looking horrified, swiftly withdrew her hands. Jed and Michael taken aback, looked at Bella as if they'd hurt her somehow.

"I'm sorry!" she croaked out crying, reaching out and holding their hands. "It's just too soon for me to be touched." Bella continued, seeing the hurt look in their eyes. Sitting down next to her Michael and Jed sat silently, as tears ran down their checks.

"We're here for you Bella. Get well." Jed stammered out.

"I love you two," Bella smiled crying.

"And we love you!" Both men said at the same time, as the room grew silent and Bella again closed her eyes.

The Interviews

Two days after Bella's arrival at the hospital, Officer Brett Hall arrived at the University for his first interview as an assistant detective. It was his dream since becoming a police officer to make detective, now, at last, he was given a chance at making it a reality. He'd been given the task of interviewing both Dean Davison and Doctor Clark over Bella's rape case, so he opted to start with Dean Johnson.

Detective Johnson, his senior, had warned him to tread carefully with both men. As he had forcefully pointed out, this was purely a part of the investigation and in no way were they suspected of being involved. Brett had spent the night working out a series of straightforward questions. He'd decided to stick to these basic questions to avoid offending either man.

Arriving at the Dean's office, Brett was offered a cup of coffee by the Dean's secretary. She informed him that the Dean, unfortunately, was running late. He'd been given an honorary award for his service to the community and had been delayed. The local member of the State Parliament who had presented it to him that morning at the Council chambers had been late, causing the problem.

Walking into the office, the Dean seeing the Officer waiting apologised for not being on time. Opening the door to his inner office, he asked Brett to come in and take a seat.

"I gather this is about Bella?" the Dean asked sounding upset.

"Yes, we're trying to find out what happened to her that night," Brett replied sitting down watching Davison closely.

"Yes, it's a mystery why she didn't turn up at our farm. I remember Doctor Clark being quite worried by her no-show. Mind you, like I told Doctor Clark, many students get stage fright when doing these recitals. I've had them not turn up on several occasions before." The Dean explained, shaking his head as if he somehow felt responsible for not taking her non-attendance more seriously. Brett watched Davison closely seeing no sign of any deceit in the Dean's story, as he wrote everything down.

"Did you see anything that night out of the ordinary?" Brett asked sorry he'd come here.

"No, I arrived home around 5 and Dr Clark at 6. He'd had a long day in surgery and had a lay down. I was to wake him when Bella arrived. When she hadn't turned up, I woke him and we had a late dinner, at about 8. We then turned in early as Dr Clark had a big day in surgery again the next day. I wish I could be more helpful."

"She said in her statement that she saw you naked, coming towards her. Why would she say that?"

"I've no idea. Sounds rather strange?" the Dean replied. He appeared to be troubled by the remark, but not in a guilty of doing something way.

"Any idea, who could've done this?"

"No, but whoever did this should be locked up. It's a sad day when you can't walk to a recital without being attacked by some monster. I wish I could help more." The Dean said sounding both angry and sincere.

"Thanks anyway Dean Davison for your time, I won't hold you up further," Brett assured him walking to the door.

"Officer if you see Bella can you send her our best, from the staff and students here." The Dean asked his face looking downcast.

"I'll do that, thanks again." Brett smiled leaving.

Behind him Davison watched him go, a small smile creasing the corners of his lips, as he tried not to laugh. 'A complete amateur,' he concluded, watching the young policeman walk to his car, still writing. Returning to his office, he rang Dr Clark, telling him word for word what he'd said, just in case the fool would-be detective bothered him. Having a quiet moment, Davison got out his I-pod deciding to listen to some music while he worked. Turning it on, he listened to his recording of Bella from the night of the recital.

She played the violin well he thought, as the violin stopped and the performance began. She didn't scream as loud as most of them had, but her muffled sobs and moans had a distinct rhythm to them he realised, as he sat thinking again of that delightful night.

When Officer Hall entered Dr Clark's office, he found Clark going over the morning's procedures with eight young doctors. These doctors had watched his morning operations and were now reviewing each one. Three were female and very attractive he noticed. After asking if he could ask him some questions, the Doctor closed the meeting, arranging to meet with them in an hour.

Officer Hall went through the standard questions finding the doctor more than happy to comply. At the end happy with the doctor's answers he asked about Bella's condition.

"Bella's been through an absolute nightmare. Whoever did this should be locked away and not released. It's a sad day when you can't walk to a recital, without being attacked by some monster." Clark answered, sounding upset.

"Thanks for your time doctor, I'll be going." Brett smiled, leaving the doctor to get on with his work.

Walking towards his car, Brett realised the doctor hadn't told him Bella's condition. Instead, he'd gone on about the safety of walking the streets. Hopping in his car, Brett thought about Clark's answer. Was the doctor angry with who had done it or was he reading out a prearranged speech, he'd made up just for Brett? Checking his statement, he noticed how similar each man's answers had been.

There was something else he remembered the Dean had said. He'd mentioned other students having stage fright and had not turned up. That meant that a lot of students had gone to Davison's home to do recitals for the two men. He made a note to track some of them down. It could be nothing, but it was his first assignment as a detective, and he wanted to make a good impression.

That afternoon Dr Clark drove home, leaving the office on time for once. Driving through town he came to a pedestrian crossing, slowing down as a young woman approached it. She was in her mid-twenties, well tanned and tall. From a surgeon's point of view, she had perfect bone structure, her body weight perfect for her height. In other words, she was beautiful and in her prime. She wore a short cut dress with a flower like pattern flowing through it, with a short blue blouse, showing off her full firm breasts

As she walked in front of his car, she smiled seductively, mouthing a thank you to him for stopping. He watched her look at his car more than impressed with the late model Mercedes. Waving to her Clark smiled, as she covered her mouth hiding her giggles indicating her interest. Driving on Clark smiled at the encounter.

He loved young women; he loved to observe them in secret when they felt safe in their homes. There they thought evil couldn't touch them as if somehow angels stood outside their doors. He watched them sometimes for weeks before he made his move. An eerie noise or a shadow outside their bedroom window is how he'd start. This gave them a taste of fear, the briefest warning, to a stranger's presence. This first contact made them catch their breath or scream in terror.

Sometimes they'd jump up, running from their room realising it wasn't as safe as they always perceived it to be. They were never sure what they'd seen or heard, but it had scared them. Fear of the unknown he suspected, always made them hesitate, before looking back out the window. Of course, by then, the cause of their alarm had disappeared, leaving them uncertain as to what they had seen.

Later they'd laugh, blaming their imagination, putting it all down to their nerves. To reassure themselves, they'd grab a torch and run to the window, or fling open the front door turning on the lights. Some even walked outside to look around. Confident again they'd return to their room, letting the falsehood of their imaginary safety enfold them once again.

When he came for them, they confronted the truth, knowing that evil had been watching them. This made their coming nightmare all the more horrendous, for their failure to protect themselves. Then the fun really started. This was when they realised there was no hope of escape, that he had them at his mercy.

Inflicting pain, watching them scream, had become like heroin to him. Rape, to him, was just another means for him to achieve his aim, of crafting an exquisite type of pain for his playthings. Sure he enjoyed releasing his seed, but it was like having an entrée without a main meal. What he craved was the power of changing their lives, recreating their very existence. They would never forget a night with him, spending the rest of their miserable lives, watching and dreading his return. They'd never be able to sleep alone, without fearing he'd wake them and their night of torment would start again.

In his passion for punishing them, some had died. It happened, unfortunately, as in his thirst for fulfilment, sometimes he went too far, losing control. Clark regretted this, as he got more pleasure from seeing them broken than actually ending their lives. Davison, on the other hand, couldn't care less what happened to them, as long as he got another. Smiling, thinking about Davison, Clark thought of a conference at the hospital earlier that year.

At the gathering, several imminent psychiatrists had tried to pin down why a man attacks and brutally rapes a woman. Most put it down to some childhood drama or trauma causing these inhuman responses. Others suggested a deep hatred of the opposite sex, triggered by some random event in their dark past. Most quoted Freud as if somehow his very name made their arguments all the more convincing. Some he remembered, even gave the impression that Freud was a distant associate, or collaborator in their theories, making their words beyond reproach.

In truth, Clark knew his addiction with inflicting pain on beautiful women, had nothing to do with their theories or interpretation. The reason why he did it, was that he liked to do it.

Bella's Recovery

Two weeks after Bella was rushed to the hospital, she managed to sit up. Recovered enough, she was moved out of Critical care to the General ward. Her legs and stomach were still a mass of stitches, causing immense pain every time she tried to move. The only bright side was they expected her to fully recover in time.

"Good morning. How is my star patient?" Doctor Douglas smiled, looking at her chart. He was more than pleased with her progress remembering what she looked like when first brought in. She defied all the odds, recovering from her ordeal, having at first been written off as beyond saving.

He'd been one of the first to see her that morning when she'd been brought in. Like the others in the Emergency Department, he'd been sickened by the damage inflicted on her. The surgical team at the hospital which he was a member of had given her zero chance of making it. To their surprise, she'd fought back making them all look like fools. It had made his day. He could still remember Doctor Clark, the head of the surgery team, arguing against surgery, considering it a waste of time.

He too had been convinced it was futile, but with another junior surgeon, Douglas had given it ago. Clark, hearing of the surgery had grinned, betting them both dinner at the best restaurant in town if they saved her. It had taken three operations over two days, but they'd pulled it off. Smiling, he remembered the look on Clark's face when he told him she was out of danger and he owed them both dinners. He was truly shocked.

Examining her face, he marvelled at her skin grafts under her chin where a long blunt instrument, maybe a whip, had cut deep into her throat. James, the junior surgeon's speciality was skin grafts, and he'd done a miracle on this girl. True there'd be scars on her back, legs and stomach, but they would fade. In a few months, there'd only be faint lines, compared to the ugly open cuts the two doctors had repaired.

What worried him was her mental state. Wounds of the body heal, phychological wounds were another matter.

She still had trouble with men touching her he observed. Even he himself, who'd saved her life, saw the fear in her eyes when he approached her. Writing on her chart to keep male staff at a distance, he lowered her pain relief, slowly weaning her off morphine.

"Keep it up young lady, because of your recovery, Doctor Clark's buying me dinner tonight." He smiled leaving. Behind him Bella stared after him, her hands trembling with fear.

Kirra like usual arrived just after the doctor had left at 7am. She didn't like Bella being on her own, so she always arrived early. The last week had been touch and go with Bella. After the second day in hospital after she'd talked to the boys, she'd gone downhill, her organs shutting down. The boys had been beside themselves with worry only to find they were barred from the hospital.

News that the police believe them responsible for her attack had spread. The hospital following the police's advice had banned them from visiting her. Heartbroken, the boys, in the end, had left it to Kirra to keep them up to date with her condition.

Entering the ward, she was surprised to see Bella sitting up. Letting out a cry of relief, Kirra rushed to her, knowing she'd finally turned a corner.

"How do you feel?" Kirra smiled, coming forward and kissing her lightly on the cheek.

"Better, for seeing you." She answered, her voice croaky, as she reached for a bottle of water with a straw in it beside her bed. Taking several mouthfuls, she put the bottle back down. "That's better. Where are Jed and Michael?" She asked, her voice sounding normal.

"Cops have had them banned from the hospital." Kirra exploded, as several nurses turned her way. "Sorry." Kirra added softly, as the nurses giving her a 'be careful look', moved on.

"That's terrible Kirra, although in a way it gives me time to be more at ease around them," Bella admitted softly, feeling she was betraying them.

"They understand. The main thing is we get you better." Kirra smiled moving on.

For the first few weeks, Bella tried just to stand up. To most people, standing up would seem straightforward. It wasn't for Bella. Her brain functions had been damaged in the beating she was given. All her body movements seemed out of sync, as her brain sent different messages to what she intended. If she tried to lift her foot, her toes would move, while when wanting to move her arms, required her to think of clenching her fingers.

She was given a slow, frustrating and repetitious group of exercises to carry out hourly, without thinking about them, doing them on instinct. In the first frustrating month, she only managed to control herself enough to stand briefly, before sitting back down. Kirra cried with joy when she saw her stand up. Bella in return, gave her a confident smile, pleased if not frustrated with her slow progress.

"That was great Bella. Now you've achieved that, there'll be no stopping you." Kirra told her hugging her.

"Yes, you're certainly a miracle. "A voice spoke from behind them, as turning, Bella saw a bunch of young Doctors standing with Doctor Clark. Bella froze unable to say anything, as Kirra not knowing who it was, smiled at the Doctor. "If you don't mind Bella, I've brought a group of students to examine you?" Doctor Clark continued, sounding very pleasant.

"I'm sorry; I didn't catch your name doctor," Kirra asked noticing Bella's look of fear.

"My name is Doctor Clark, I'm the head surgeon here. You can call me Robert if you wish." He smiled. Kirra at first failed to connect the dots, till suddenly she remembered the name.

"No, you haven't got permission to go near her. So get the fuck away!" Kirra told him, looking him straight in the eye. The young students with him, looked at her as if she'd turned into a rabid dog.

"There is no call for that language, young lady. I will take the students elsewhere.' Clark replied, appearing shocked by her reply.

"Go before I call a nurse," Bella said from her bed, as the group moved away. Kirra once they'd left, broke down sobbing. Bella holding her hand comforted her.

"That vile evil creature! To come near you after what he did." Kirra sobbed, trying to pull herself back together.

"He's playing a game with me Kirra. He wants me to know he can come for me when he likes." Bella explained, her eyes glistening with tears.

"We've got to tell someone!"

"Who can we tell Kirra? Men like Clark own this town. We're trash to most people who live here." Bella whispered, seeing the way the people around them had reacted to Kirra swearing at the doctor.

"We've got to get you out of here as soon as possible." Kirra put forward, watching the door.

"You're right Kirra, I'm not safe here," Bella said softly sounding scared.

For the next three months Kirra watched over Bella every day, only leaving to clean up and sleep before returning. Her wounds though severe, slowly healed, the stitches removed periodically. For some reason, her attackers had only done superficial damage to her breasts and thighs, as if saving those areas for their own pleasure. In a way, it was a good thing the doctors pointed out. Even though she'd be badly scarred, they assured her she would mend, and be able to have children.

Bella greeted this so-called blessing with silence as pain racked her body. She knew why they'd left her breasts and thighs untouched. They intended to abduct and rape her again. That's how they got their kicks, she realized. It wasn't the rape that turned them on; it was the fear their prey felt, waiting for them to come for them again.

Her mind, unfortunately, was still muddled, unable to clearly tell her what had occurred. When she'd broached her memory problem with the doctors, they were unable to tell her if she would ever remember. They sighted the number of drugs in her system and the emotional shock from the attack. 'Give it time' they all said, patting her on the shoulder reassuringly. Time regrettably was one thing she didn't have. Unlike her doctors, she knew her predators were watching her every move.

As the weeks past, her scars slowly faded, as did the terror that filled the dark when she tried to sleep. At first, she was worried, that Clark might try to finish her while she slept in hospital. In time she realised the nurses were always there after dark, locking down the area she was in. This gave her some comfort, because at any other time during the day, Kirra was there. It didn't mean she wasn't scared.

At the hospital and later at the farm, she would always sleep with the light on, unable to stand the darkness and what lurked there. Many at the hospital thought she'd never recover from the trauma she'd been through. She surprised them all mostly due to the love her friends showered on her in the months she spent recovering.

During Bella's recovery, her three friends lived with another problem. They had become social outcast in the area, finding no one wanted to be near them. As word spread about the attack, the police let it be known who they thought was responsible. Going out for Michael and

Jed became dangerous. At first, there was the odd ugly look or the word 'Rapist' yelled from passing cars.

Then the local markets where they sold their produce refused them a stall, citing lack of space. After they threatened the market with court action, they again were allowed to attend, only to find their stall vandalised with the word 'Rapist' scrolled all over it. In the end, it wasn't worth going anyway, as customers avoided their stall as if they were lepers. This forced them to sell elsewhere at a lower price, which in turn, forced both Jed and Kirra onto the dole.

Death threats by anonymous callers to get out of town or else filled their message recorder. It forced them to cut their phone off, relying on their mobiles, which had caller recognition. Several times their crops were set on fire, the police turning a blind eye to their complaints. To make matters worse, suddenly everyone was after them.

From the tax department to social security, everyone wanted a piece of them. Driving to the hospital became a ritual of being pulled over and searched. The car itself defected several times. In the end, they purchased bikes being the only way to get around, leaving Michael's vehicle at home. Twice the boys were sideswiped by cars on the way to town, ending up in a ditch beside it. Luckily they were not harmed, but the message was clear.

Even going to the local pub became dangerous for both Michael and Jed. Several times they had a run in with some of the locals, getting severely beaten. Even the alternative groups, whom once thought Michael was a hero, avoided them. In the end, the only thing that kept them going was their love for each other.

THE HOMECOMING

It was over six months from the night of the recital when Bella returned home to the farm. Her parents furious over Bella's backing of the boys gave her an ultimatum. 'Have nothing to do with Jed and Michael and come home, or don't come home at all'. Sadly she refused to give up her friends, telling her parents to show some Christian charity.

Instead, they left her clothes and belongings at the hospital, without speaking to Bella. Being abandoned by her family gutted her spiritually, only Kirra's and the boys' constant support and her entrenched faith upheld her.

Driving Bella home, Michael sat stone-faced not knowing what to say to her. Bella had gone from a happy chatterbox to nearly mute, hardly talking at all. As if feeling his concern, Bella placed her hand on his thigh, resting it lightly there reassuring him.

"Give me time Michael," Bella whispered, as he silently nodded his understanding.

Turning onto the farm road, Bella looked towards the farmhouse, to see Kirra and Jed standing waiting for them. Michael nosed his old Ute up next to the front door, allowing her to step straight onto the front veranda stairs.

"Welcome home!" Kirra and Jed shouted, hugging their friend lightly, as a silence developed, with Bella not answering.

"She's tired, let's get her inside," Michael suggested softly, the others nodding their support, as her gear was unloaded.

Two weeks after Bella's homecoming, Jed made a discovery. His supply of 'Ice' tablets had mysteriously halved. At first, he thought he'd taken them without thinking in one of his less than cognizant moments. Becoming worried he might be tripping out and using up his supply, he had Michael monitor them. Two nights afterwards he found Kirra dipping into Jed's supply.

"What are you doing Kirra?" Michael asked watching her guiltily stash the tablets into her pocket.

"I just need something to sleep."

"Not that amount!" Jed exploded, from the door.

"It's for me as well," Bella confessed, moving into view from the bedroom, which she was sharing with Kirra at the moment. Since Bella's return, the two girls had become like shadows, keeping to themselves, alienating the men.

"This is not the answer!" Jed sobbed. "Look at me, look what I've become. Do you really think it will take away the pain?" He screamed grabbing the tablets from Kirra.

"Give them back!" She shrieked, slapping him, making the room freeze. "I'm sorry Jed. I don't know what happened." Kirra whispered crying, as Bella ran forward holding her.

Michael stood in disbelief. Tears started flowing down his face, as the reality of Kirra and Bella using hit him. He couldn't believe they could do something so stupid after seeing what Jed had been through. Unable to look at them any longer, Michael walked out the front door into the night.

The three watched him go, as their shared shame, had made time itself slow. They realised that their friendship had reached a crossroad. Kirra could not find the words to stop him. Instead, she hung her head in humiliation.

"Michael, please don't go!" Bella cried out, begging him to stay. Instead, he kept going, his shoulders shaking as he sobbed, unable to look at them. Time dragged by as Kirra, Bella and Jed fought to find something to say to each other. Bella in the end spoke.

"I was trying to forget the pain." This made Jed turn back from watching the doorway. Jed had just witnessed the friend who'd saved him from certain death; see two of his other friends head down the same path.

"Do you two think it somehow makes what you've fucking done more acceptable?" Jed said, his face and voice, changing from shame to anger.

"Who are you to talk?" Kirra shot back, her eyes glazing over as she took on a feral demeanour.

"Stop it, stop it! Bella screeched, holding her head trying to stop the thumping, wanting a pill desperately. Looking towards his pocket, she moved towards him, as Jed's arms shot out, stopping her. Grabbing Kirra as well, he half dragged, half carried them, towards their room. Shoving them both inside, he grabbed the key from their side of the lock, slamming the door. Swiftly he locked it on his side as the two women beat against the door.

"Open this door you fucking dope head bastard!" Kirra shouted, as Jed wiping his eyes moved outside. Both girls continued to yell and scream as Jed sat down next to Michael.

"I couldn't stay in there Jed, I'm sorry."

"There's nothing for you to be sorry about Michael. I brought the drugs into this house, I'll handle it."

"Will they be okay?"

"I'm not sure. I don't think they've taken enough to get a hold on them, like it has me. I'll keep them locked up for a few days, and then we'll see."

"They sound pretty pissed!"

"It's just the start Michael. Going cold turkey is a bitch. In a few days, we should know one way or the other if they've made it." Jed admitted as the two friends sat in silence, listening to the screaming inside. Michael felt out of his depth as the girls begged him to let them out. He'd been through something similar with Jed although he had been strong enough then to resist the urge to let him out. In the end, he'd been forced to take him to the hospital, after his attempt to break free had failed, nearly killing him.

Now listening to the girls scream, he wondered if he could stand going through it again. The sound of breaking glass made them both jump, as the girls' bedroom window crashed outside from their room. Running around outside their home Jed and Michael found Kirra trying to climb out their window. Shoving her back inside, Jed watched the window, while Michael fetched some planks and nails. Swiftly nailing up the opening, the two men retreated to the veranda, followed by abuse from the girls.

"That was close," Michael admitted shaking with pent-up emotion.

"It's going to be a long couple of days I can tell you," Jed replied his hands shaking as well.

"I've got confidence in you, Jed, to look after them," Michael whispered, walking off into the dark to think.

Once away from Jed, Michael vomited, emptying his stomach. He really felt like leaving, taking the coward's way out and bolting. In the end, coming to his senses, he walked back; knowing everything he loved was here. Jed was still sitting on the veranda, staring into the darkness, as the howling continued. Seeing Michael, Jed passed him a beer, as they both sat silently, the yelling from inside slowly subsiding.

After a week of absolute hell, Jed released the girls from their room. The only thing allowed into their room for the past week was food and water, and the only reason they left was to go to the toilet, supervised. The smell of the room and the girls was overwhelming; the first thing they both asked for was a shower. While the girls cleaned themselves, Jed and Michael worked in their room, throwing out the soiled bed linen.

No one talked at dinner that night, as shame gripped the group. Both girls, in the end, expressed thanks to Jed, before guiltily retiring to their room. Sitting on the veranda, Michael thanked Jed for his tireless effort in helping the girls.

"We were lucky Michael, it could've gone the other way," Jed whispered not wanting the girls to know how close it had been. Michael could see that despite his attempt to play it down, Jed was thrilled. He'd managed to break them both away from the nightmare that held him, and in a way repent some of his sins.

Over the next two months, Bella slowly improved, gaining the trust that had been ripped away from her. Kirra's support was everything, though the drug problem had shown them how vulnerable they were too quick fixes. Time was what Bella needed, and answers to what had happened to her.

Brett, the young police officer, came several times; keeping them informed as to what was going on. It wasn't great news, all her samples from the hospital, were inconclusive, having been tainted by a foreign agent, rendering them useless. He'd been to see Dean Davison and Doctor Clark. Both had been home that night together, waiting for Bella to turn up.

When she hadn't shown, they put it down to nerves; they seemed quite concerned about what happened. No one seemed to know anything, but he'd keep digging.

"Waste of time, no one's going to believe Bella." Jed pointed out to Michael after Officer Hall had left.

"You can see their point, Jed. Even Bella's not sure." Michael reminded him.

"Someone knows, it's about time we did some digging of our own." Jed put forward, staring out over the valley.

"So what are you suggesting?" Michael asked apprehensively.

"We could look around the Dean's house," Jed
suggested.

"I can't go to jail Jed, I would rather be dead," Michael
whispered sounding scared.

"Either could I without my pills Michael. But we've got
to do something to help Bella! We just can't let whoever
did this get away with it." Jed growled.

"How about the two of you retrace her steps, maybe
you'll find something?" Kirra put forward from the
doorway, having listened to the boys talking.

"It could be dangerous Kirra. We're not exactly popular
at the moment." Jed said softly, hoping Bella wasn't
listening as well.

"First we'll ask Bella, what she remembers. We need
to get as much information from her as possible. Then
we've got to search, there's got to be something or
someone who can give us a clue, as to what happened."
Kirra proposed, knowing that including Bella was
important.

"It won't hurt to try, but it's been a long time." Michael
pointed out, the others sadly agreeing.

THE SEARCH

After getting Bella's shaky approval, Jed and Michael retraced the route Bella took that night. It was around 10 in the morning, and being a workday meant both the Dean and the Doctor wouldn't be home. Peddling along Jed and Michael looked for any signs that would help them, knowing more than eight months had elapsed, leaving the trail cold. Reaching the main town, Jed signalled Michael to pull over and get a drink.

Short of funds they decided on the church drop-in centre, run by the ex-biker priest. Grabbing a free lemon drink, they both sat down on the steps of the church relaxing in the sun. Pessimistic at the hunt so far, Jed looked up to see the priest watching them. Ambling over, he seated himself beside them.

"How's Bella?" Ben asked neutrally.

"She's a lot better, but it's going to take her some time to fully recover father," Michael answered honestly.

"Any clues as to what happened?" the Priest asked softly. Michael and Jed regarded the priest with respect, knowing he was one of the rare people who believed them.

"Nothing, unfortunately, even the cops have drawn a blank. We're retracing her path to the Dean's house, trying to find something to work with." Michael volunteered, the priest nodding his understanding.

"You know I saw her that night," the Priest admitted thinking back. "She came down the same way as you did now, then turned at the fork up ahead going north over the bridge. Mind you, it's the quickest way to the Dean's home." the Priest informed them.

"God, you're the first person we know who saw her that night!" Jed replied excitedly, knowing now that she had gone to the Dean's house.

"Well let's hope he's helping you." The priest smiled, at Jed's reference to God.

"Thanks, father, you've been a great help, we'll keep going." Michael smiled, as they hurried back to their bikes.

"Be careful both of you." The Priest warned. He knew they'd been blamed for the attack on Bella and a lot of people had it in for them."

"We will father," Jed replied a small grin on his face as Michael stopped turning.

"Why do you believe we're innocent while everyone else doesn't?"

"I have a gift for reading people Michael. You are all in love with each other I can see that. It mightn't be the stereotype between man and woman, but it's love, just the same. That's why I know that you are both incapable of hurting Bella." The priest answered walking away.

"You know I never saw Bella's thing for God, but that man is something special isn't he?" Jed whispered to Michael.

"Yeah makes you wonder how a tough biker gives up his lifestyle to do what he does now," Michael replied, hopping on his bike and starting to pedal. Riding off with renewed vigour, both Michael and Jed, for the first time in the last 8 months, felt like they were getting somewhere.

"Those two are the rapists, aren't they? What are they doing hanging around our church?" An old woman asked from behind the priest.

"They're not rapist my dear. And that aside, anyone is welcome in God's house" Ben the Priest replied, forcing a smile. He knew how the rumours had spread about the two boys throughout the area.

"The police think they are!" The woman answered gruffly.

"If the police thought they'd done it, they'd have arrested them. Let's go pray that God helps the police find these evil men who are responsible." Ben suggested.

Watching them ride towards the bridge, the priest prayed that God would help them. They certainly needed it.

Riding past the Dean's front gate Jed and Michael, felt a little scared, as they continued on making sure no one was around. Doubling back, they dismounted about fifty metres further down the road stretching their legs. Making sure no one was following them; they hid their bikes, walking back to the entrance. The Dean's house somehow looked sinister to Michael. Even though he was sure no one was home, he had the feeling it was watching them, hoping to trap and imprison them both.

"Keep outside the fence line, we don't want any trouble," Michael whispered to Jed as if the house was listening.

"We'll walk beside the hedge. That way we're not on their property, and it will help keep us out of sight." Jed replied leading. Turning to walk along the boundary next to the hedge, Jed had only taken a few steps when he suddenly froze. Michael scared, was just about to ask what was wrong, when he too spotted Bella's bike.

Both stood silently, looking at the bike as if seeing an apparition. It was leaning against the hedge and was badly rusted. Covered with new growth as the hedge expanded out into the adjoining field, it had become part of it.

"She was here, those bastards were lying!" Jed exploded his fist clenching.

"Settle down Jed; let's go see that young cop," Michael suggested, his eyes glued to the bike.

"Waste of time Michael. We know now the Dean's involved and Bella made it here." Jed erupted.

"That's not proof Jed! She could've been grabbed here, by someone else, though it seems unlikely." Michael admitted. Jed angrily turned to face Michael, he was about to explode, wanting his friend to back him and kill these bastards. Looking into Michael's eyes, he saw the only person who had helped him when he was dying, and his anger fled.

"Okay, we'll do it your way," Jed whispered, turning back towards their bikes to hide his anger.

Michael watched Jed knowing that look. He knew Jed was about to suggest another course of action when he nodded his acceptance. Michael felt he knew what he wanted to do; hoping that this course of action he'd suggested worked instead. He was no murderer he realised, as they both peddled back towards the police station.

Officer Brett Hall sat typing his way through a mountain of reports. Making detective was not the walk in the park he'd been told. He thought he'd be mostly out arresting scumbags. Instead, he was finishing yet another report into a missing vehicle, reportedly stolen. Times were tuff at the moment and this vehicle, which once had been the treasured procession of a young family, now was a burnout wreck. The owners, who could only just afford it, were now the prime suspects in the vehicle's demise.

Brett had interviewed both the husband and wife finding them overly nervous. Benny, the husband, had lost his job and his wife was again pregnant with their third child. Why had the finance company given them a loan in the first place? The thought really pissed him off. They must've known they couldn't afford it even with him employed. They were insured for just enough to cover paying off the car, so he'd figured to get out of debt and save their house, they'd torch the car.

He then checked out the car yard where they'd bought it, finding they'd been sold a lemon, it's price way above its resale value. This made it impossible for them to even try selling it, trapping them even more. He had examined the burnt-out remains of the vehicle himself, finding the ignition key still in the ignition. This was a sure sign that it hadn't been stolen.

Thinking about the young family, he made a decision. Throwing the key into the bin, he signed off on the report, that the vehicle had been stolen, by persons unknown. Sending the father to jail and throwing the family out into the street wasn't going to help anyone. He knew he'd broken the rules, but the car yard and the finance company were just as much to blame.

After work today he'd go back to the couple's house and read them the riot act, warning them that next time they'd be in for it. He hoped it would help, he knew he could live with his decision on this one.

His thoughts were interrupted when the constable from the desk informed him that the suspected rapists Jed and Michael were asking for him. Puzzled, the new detective stood up, walking to the front desk.

"What's up?" Brett asked as both Jed and Michael answered at the same time.

"One at a time thanks!" Brett asked abruptly, his dislike for them plain to see. At first, the two men hesitated, as if thinking it was a waste of time telling Brett anything, Michael finally spoke.

"We found Bella's bike beside the boundary hedge, bordering the Dean's house!" Michael informed him, waiting.

"How do I know you didn't place it there?" Brett asked watching their reaction.

"Let's go, Michael!" Jed snarled, turning to the door.

"Settle down Jed," Michael ordered, turning back to Brett. "We decided to trace Bella's movements. We came through town stopping at the outreach church. The priest said he saw Bella on the night take the bridge leading to the Dean's house. We then rode there, finding Bella's bike beside the side hedge, she must have put it there out of sight." Michael stated, watching Brett's reaction.

"Okay, let's go look," Brett suggested giving them a small smile, knowing they both disliked each other. Grabbing a set of keys from behind the desk he led them outside to a police car, much to the surprise of Michael and Jed.

Driving back out to the Dean's house, in the front of a police car for a change, was an interesting experience for Jed and Michael. No one talked, all locked in their own thoughts at what this meant. Brett was secretly excited, having exhausted all leads on Bella's case. He'd tried over the last few weeks to track down any students who had been at the Dean's house for recitals.

Of the twenty over the last year, eight were male the others female. All the males he'd tracked down, finding they'd had no problems at the house. The females were a different story. Six were overseas and were unable to be contacted, or didn't want to talk.

Of the six that remained here, five had committed suicide, the remaining one he hadn't been able to find yet. The suicide thing worried him, why so high in this group of young women? The parents he'd talked to were unaware of any problems. Most didn't want to talk about it. Brett had a bad feeling about it, but no evidence, until now.

Arriving at the property, Jed led the detective to Bella's bike. It was where they said it was and the ground hadn't been disturbed, showing it had been there for some time. Taking several photographs he carefully wrapped the bike in plastic, putting it in the police car.

"And the priest saw her riding out here that night?" Brett asked them again, getting silent nods in return.

"Okay, I'll look into it, don't say anything to anyone. Okay?" Brett said softly.

"Who would believe us?" Jed replied sadly, as Brett drove them back to the police station.

"Thanks for going out there with us," Michael said to Brett getting out of the car, moving towards their bikes.

"Look I mightn't like you two, but for the record, I believe you. And don't go near Davison and Clark again. Leave the investigating to us, okay." Brett suggested forcefully, getting a subdued acceptance from Jed and Michael as they rode away.

After Jed and Michael had departed, Brett went to see the priest. When he walked into the church, several parishioners decided to make themselves scarce, making him smile. The Priest seeing the exit of his followers spotted Brett.

"Hard to save them, when they run like that." He smiled, offering his hand.

"Detective Hall, but you can call me Brett."

"The name's Ben, what's the problem?"

Brett told him about what Jed and Michael had found and that they had told him, he'd seen Bella that night. Ben confirmed their story assuring the detective what they said was true. Taking a statement, Brett recorded everything, his excitement building.

"You think the Dean and Dr Clark are responsible?" Ben said softly.

"Yes, although proving it, is the hard thing." Brett sense, that the priest knew something. "Is there something else you can tell me, Ben?"

"Unfortunately I can't help detective. I've taken confessions from some young ladies in the area over the years. I think you could be onto something."

"Can you give me more than that?"

"No I can't, as much as I wish I could."

"Are you saying they raped other women?"

"No nothing like that. It's just, a couple thought they'd seen one of these gentlemen at night, outside their homes. I can't say any more than that, I've said too much already." Ben replied looking ashamed, knowing he'd broken a sacred trust already.

"Thanks anyway father. What you told me won't be written down." Brett assured him leaving.

The priest watched him go, feeling terrible. Two girls had told him that Clark was following them. They'd told the priest not as a supposed threat, but as a temptation, thinking by sleeping with him, they could advance their careers. He warned them to remain strong and resist the temptation.

Now he realised these two girls could've been intended victims, but in seeing Clark following them, had made him back off. It was the one thing about the confession he hated. Knowing the guilty were getting away with their crimes and at the same time not being able to act. He'd just broken that sacred trust, in talking to the young officer, if not in a roundabout way.

Sometimes God does work in mysterious ways he smiled, putting it down to divine intervention.

Breaking Free

Back home the discovery of the bike was greeted with a lukewarm response. Bella went to her room crying, while Kirra sat silently feeling guilty that she had doubted Bella. Jed wanted to do something immediately. Michael thought it prudent to wait to see what the cops did.

"The cop won't do anything! We've got to take care of those two perverts!" Jed growled, clenching his fist.

"The young cop believes us, let's give him time. I know how you feel mate, but killing Clark and Davison, isn't going to help Bella." Michael pleaded. Kirra shocked, nodded her support.

"Okay Michael, but I think you're wrong," Jed whispered moving off, walking out onto the farm.

"He won't do anything stupid will he?" Kirra asked sounding scared.

"No, not yet, but I see his point. There's a good chance those two monsters will get off. There's just not enough evidence." Michael admitted as Kirra sat down beside him, holding his hand.

Bella lay in her room listening to her friends discuss what to do. Up till this point, she'd thought maybe her memories were faulty, that she was losing it. This information proved she wasn't insane, as the bonds of depression that had held her since that night, started to break, freeing her. Jed was angry, mainly because like the others he at first thought she had lost it. Now he felt guilty and wanted to strike out. His anger would fade with time she hoped, as she got out of bed and stretched feeling better than she had for a long time.

Dinner that night was the first where Bella had joined in the conversation, even laughing. Kirra spent most of the night hiding tears that flowed down her face at Bella's return from her self-imposed exile. Michael and Jed were just relieved to see her smile again, knowing somehow their escapade today had helped. Since the hospital, Bella had slept with Kirra in her room, keeping their two lovers at a distance. This had hurt them, more than the police beatings, as they somehow felt responsible for her attack.

With this change in her, the men hoped that soon they could again share their beds with their lovers, reconfirming their love for each other. Kirra missed the men's companionship as well. Staying with Bella to support her had cut her link with the men as well. She loved making love, revelling in the passion they all shared. Somehow she knew that making love without Bella was a betrayal, so she had abstained, hoping to in some way support her. She knew this denial had made them all unhappy, something she regretted.

Lying there alone that night in bed, Michael wished that Bella or Kirra would join him. It had been too long, and he missed their lovemaking. Like Jed, he felt the loneliness of their emotional bond being severed.

"At least there's hope now," Michael whispered.

WENDY

Detective Hall should have felt on top of the world. He'd made detective, a lifelong dream had been achieved, so why wasn't he celebrating? The Bella case sat on his desk, unfinished. He'd been given the 'It's overdue' speech from his boss, pointing out that a new detective should have closed it swiftly. The other detectives mainly Johnson, were convinced it was the two druggies she lived with. Brett knew if he pointed the finger at Jed and Michael, it would close the file, making things neater for him. The problem was with Bella refusing to testify against Jed and Michael, made taking them to court nearly impossible. With the finding of the bike, Brett had started digging again.

His visit to Ben the priest had confirmed what Michael had said. Ben had also revealed, off the record, that Clark or the Dean had been stalking other girls. It was like a giant jigsaw puzzle, making no sense till every piece was in place. Making a decision, Brett decided to take a chance and return to the hospital. He hoped to shake something loose from Doctor Clark; he seemed the less formable of the two.

Doctor Clark, Head of Surgery was a hard man to get an appointment with. It took three attempts to arrange an interview, and even then when Brett turned up the Doctor was in surgery. In the end, Brett cornered him having lunch. Pulling up a chair opposite Doctor Clark in the Surgeons' cafeteria, Brett sensed an undercurrent of anger by his presence. If it was to do with the case or disturbing the good doctor's lunch, Brett wasn't sure, but he found the show of anger interesting.

"Sorry to intrude Doctor, but I'm having trouble getting a meeting with you," Brett informed him.

"Well it must be important to disturb my lunch, so what's the problem?" Clark answered smiling.

"It's about the Bella case," Brett told him watching him closely.

"Oh, that poor girl how is she," Clark asked sounding genuinely sincere.

"Good, she's recovering well. The problem is there are a few matters I need to clear up." Brett replied.

"I've already told you she didn't reach our home. What else is there?" Clark asked, his smile never leaving his lips.

"We have a witness who saw her riding to your home. We also found her bike near your front gate, meaning she did, in fact, make it there." As Brett watched Clark, he saw the doctor's eyes take on a sinister quality, even though the smile remained on his lips. For several seconds, Clark sat staring at the detective, before answering.

"Someone must have grabbed her from out front or the drugs she'd taken made her abandon the bike and walk away without it," Clark answered slowly, thinking before speaking.

"Funny they would just happen past when she arrived there?" Brett replied.

"Are you suggesting something else detective?" Clark asked his voice laced with suppressed anger.

"Not yet. I've got a theory | just need a bit more evidence." Brett smiled. "Thanks for your time doctor, you've been most helpful," he added as he stood and walked away.

Clark sat watching the detective leave, his anger ready to explode. Closing his eyes, he allowed his anger to dissipate. Picking up his mobile, he rang Davison. Explaining the situation, Davison suggested a solution, as Clark hanging up, rang the local Police Superintendent.

Brett walked through the hospital going over the interview. Clark was dangerous Brett mused, remembering his eyes. He's guilty, Brett knew it now, but what should he do? Turning a corner not paying attention, the detective collided with a nurse.

"God, I'm sorry!" Brett blurted out, as he stared at the nurse's long legs.

"That's okay I've had worst done to me here." The Nurse smiled, straightening her clothing.

"You're the nurse who looked after Bella aren't you?" Brett asked, remembering the attractive young woman.

"Yes, I was on duty when she arrived. I didn't catch your name?" The nurse bluntly replied, studying Brett.

"I'm Detective Brett Hall, I'm handling the case. You can call me Brett." He told her, showing his badge.

"My name's Wendy. And yes I was looking after her, although we don't usually give out information on a patient." Wendy informed him.

"Can I buy you a cup of coffee, to make up for knocking you over? I've also got some questions about the case, not the patient if that's okay?" Brett answered.

"Yeah sure, there's a cafeteria at the rear of the hospital, we can have one there," Wendy suggested. Together they walked towards the cafeteria, swapping small talk about their jobs. Behind them, Dr Clark having just finished his phone call watched this new development with a slight sense of fear. He knew the nurse could connect him with the DNA samples. Picking up his phone again, he called Davison arranging to meet to discuss this new development.

Purchasing two coffees, Brett brought them over to the table Wendy had commandeered in the busy cafeteria. Sitting down Brett sipped his coffee studying Wendy. She was quite striking in her uniform, and Brett like most men tried to imagine her without it.

"Weren't you going to ask me some questions?"
Wendy asked.

"Yes of course." Brett stammered choking on his
coffee, making Wendy giggle. "Sorry, my mind was on
something else."

"I bet it was" Wendy replied guessing, making Brett
hesitate.

"Anyway, let's get down to business," Brett suggested
moving on from his blunder. "At the moment, my
detective friends think Bella's two boyfriends are
involved. I think it's someone else, but the evidence is
pretty thin. So if you've got anything or saw anything, it
would be a big help." Brett asked softly, making sure he
wasn't overheard.

"Bella thought it was the Dean. She told me, she saw
him naked." Wendy whispered looking around as well.

"Yeah she told us that too, but evidence points to two
men involved," Brett replied softly conveying someone
else she knew.

"There was one other thing. That afternoon, after Bella
arrived at the hospital, I was finishing up my shift and
went to change in our locker room at the rear of the
hospital. When I came out to leave, I saw Dr Clark next to
the police evidence box. It's where DNA and other
evidence of a case are secured until they go away to the
forensic lab for testing. He wasn't actually touching the
evidence box, but he was wearing gloves at the time,
which was unusual." Wendy whispered nervously.

Brett sat there taken aback by her statement. This tied
Clark to the case, even though it was flimsy.

"Would he have access?" Brett whispered this time.

"Yes, all Doctors do." She admitted her eyes going
wide as she saw Dr Clark walk into the cafeteria, before
lining up at the food counter. Seeing her suddenly freeze,
Brett turned around spotting Clark at the counter.

"Relax he's just getting something to eat," Brett suggested smiling.

"Let's go." She said nervously, getting up and walking towards the front exit, causing Brett to stand and leave as well. Silence settled over the pair, as Wendy walked quickly to her car, radiating fear.

"Wendy you've got nothing to worry about. It was just a coincidence that he walked in." Brett assured her.

"No, it wasn't! Surgeons have their own eating area, they don't eat with the rest of us!" Wendy replied sounding frightened.

"It's okay," Brett assured her hugging her beside the car. "Give me your address and number, we'll talk later." Brett continued, getting a smile.

"Okay, but you're sure this is about the case." Wendy giggled.

"See you're better already." Brett smiled.

"It's just since Bella was here and I saw him near the evidence box, he's been watching me. The guy gives me the creeps." Wendy admitted, getting into her car.

"I'll ring you soon," Brett promised as she drove off giving him a wave. Looking back towards the hospital Brett for a second thought he saw Clark watching from the corner of the building, before disappearing. Blinking, seeing no one, Brett put it down to nerves, as he walked back to his car.

Standing next to his vehicle, Brett about to open it stopped. Thinking back to the cafeteria, he remembered Clark had already had lunch when he'd interviewed him earlier. That meant he had been following him. Sitting down inside his car, Brett pondered how much he could push this case. Clark, he knew now was guilty, it was proving it. He was just about to turn on the ignition when his phone rang.

"Hello, Detective Hall here."

"Brett, its Inspector Hayes can you come straight back here, we need a talk." the Inspector said bluntly, hanging up.

"Shit, what's that about?" Brett asked himself, driving back to the station.

Walking to the Inspector's office, Brett knocked then waited.

"Get in here Detective!" Inspector Hayes yelled from inside the office. Brett mystified by the tone entered. "What the fuck are you doing accusing a leading citizen of being involved in a rape case!" the Inspector exploded, stunning Brett. He came to a conclusion that Clark must have rung the Inspector, which made Brett see red.

"I did nothing of the sort. I questioned him on the bike of the victim being found near his house." Brett answered angrily.

"Keep away from Dr Clark, unless you've got some bloody solid evidence. Is that understood detective?" the Inspector barked, pointing at the door. Brett without another word left, slamming the door in a silent protest.

Arriving back at his desk, he found Detective Johnson and Detective Luke waiting.

"You couldn't let it go could ya?" Dave chuckled, making Ross smile.

"I'm doing my fucking job; you should try it one day!" Brett spat out, as both Detective Johnson and Luke lost their smiles.

"Watch your mouth detective! Remember who you're talking to." Dave snapped back at him, going toe to toe with Brett.

"Why are you rocking the boat, Brett? You know we've got those two losers for this attack." Ross asked seriously, trying to cool down his two associates.

"Call it a gut feeling if you like, but the more I dig, the dirtier Clark and Davison look.

"What evidence have you got?" Dave smirked, watching Brett's hands ball into fists.

"One, most of the girls who went to do private recitals at the Dean's house have either committed suicide or gone overseas not wanting to talk. Two, yesterday Jed and Michael led me to Bella's bike beside the Dean's house. I examined it, and it hadn't been planted there, it had been there a long time. Three, a local priest confirmed he saw Bella going through town to the Dean's house that night. He also let slip that the two have been following other women.

Four, the nurse on duty saw Dr Clark near the evidence box with gloves on. I'm going to send a request to forensics to see if the DNA was inconclusive or tampered with. Five, when I talked to Clark, I saw something dangerous in his eyes." Brett put in plain words, waiting for Johnson to answer. Both senior detectives looked at each other before answering.

"I admit there's something strange there, but your evidence is too weak, most is circumstantial," Dave answered; still, sure those two dropkicks had done it.

"Let him run with it, Dave. Let's see if he gets his arse kicked!" Ross suggested, secretly thinking Brett might have something. Dave paced back and forth, thinking. In the end, he made a decision.

"Okay run with it smartarse. But keep away from Clark and Davison, unless you've got enough to charge them with. Are we clear?" Johnson exclaimed, seeing Brett's hands relax.

"Okay, I've got one woman to track down who did a recital, plus the forensics answer. I won't go near them until I'm sure." Brett agreed as his two associates left.

Walking back to their desks Ross voiced his concerns.

"Look, Dave, I know the kids green, but he's got something."

"Yeah, you're right, something's not quite right. Bella's bike at the Dean's house worries me. Those two dropkicks still could have placed it there after the rape, but it seems a bit complicated for them. I just don't see Clark and Davison doing it. Why would they rape some druggie's whore, when every female in town is trying to let them into their pants? With the money they've got, they could have anyone I just don't see it. Anyway, let's see how our young friend goes." Dave replied bluntly.

"He's feisty when he's angry! I thought he was going to deck you when he came in." Ross admitted grinning.

"Yeah, I thought he was too. Maybe he has what it takes to be a detective." Dave chuckled.

After Johnson and Detective Luke had left, Brett sat thinking about the case. He had a feeling Ross at least believed him after he told him of the evidence, though Dave was right that it was circumstantial. The case hung on the forensic evidence and the missing girl. Each on its own was nothing, but if the evidence had been deliberately tampered with and the girl had something to tell them about her recital, it could tie everything together.

First things first, Brett decided to send for the forensic check into the samples sent, asking for an examination to see if they were deliberately rendered useless. The answer Brett knew could take weeks, maybe months, but if the results were positive to tampering, it was worth it. The second was finding the girl. He had her name. All he needed was a place to search for her.

All efforts in the police's database had come up empty, as well as government records. He knew she hadn't left the country, so where was she? In doubt, he decided to visit Ross maybe he knew another way of looking. Walking into Ross's office, Brett stared at the untidy mess that was the Detective's desk.

"Given up already?" Ross smiled.

"Got a question for you, Detective!" Brett asked ignoring Ross' remark.

"Shoot! And call me Ross He replied becoming serious. Brett told him how the girl had dropped off the grid, wondering if he had any ideas.

"Could be she's in protective custody or the Feds have her. She may be being held for her own safety in a mental institution. Those three places may be worth a try, even though the first two are highly unlikely. I'd go with the third, by the high amount of suicides you talked about." Ross concluded.

"That's great, I never thought of that, thanks," Brett replied.

"See us old guys know a few things." Ross laughed as Brett hurried out. Getting back to his office, Brett put out a bulletin to all institutions informing them that the girl was needed in an ongoing investigation. This he hoped would shake something loose. Having covered all the bases, his mind went back to Wendy. He decided he needed to ask her more questions, maybe over dinner, he decided smiling, as he rung her number.

Behind him, Ross sat looking at the door. This case had made him constantly think of his missing daughter. When kidnapped, she'd been the same age as Bella. At first, he'd been convinced it was those two dickheads she lived with, that had attacked her. Now with Brett's new investigation, he wasn't sure. Giving them that belting in the cell had made him remember his daughter's killers were still out there. Maybe that's why he'd laid into them so violently, somehow wanting to punish them for his daughter.

There wasn't a day that went by when Ross didn't think of his daughter or see her in his nightmares. She was his only child, a good kid who had enjoyed life. When they'd been told she'd been kidnapped, his wife had fallen to pieces. Ross in desperation had promised her he'd find her. It was a stupid thing to do, but at the time he thought with the whole force behind him, he'd succeed. After a year of intensive enquiries and dead-end leads, the Police admitted defeat, and with that, his wife left him.

Broken having nowhere to go, he drowned himself in alcohol, in the end being suspended. After another year of self-pity, Ross awoke to find Dave at his door. Taking no bullshit from him, Dave had taken him to his home, sobering him up. Two months on, found him back working, assisting Dave to clean up the area of undesirables.

Catching scumbags had become his main focus for living, hoping someday to find that one clue that would lead him to his daughter's killers. His only description of them was they'd been in their late thirties, in an old brown van. That cleared Michael and Jed, though the age fitted Davison and Clark.

"You're jumping at shadows?" he told himself out loud, thinking the connection thin, as he returned to his work.

PLAYTHINGS

Clark and Davison sat in their favourite restaurant, sipping a glass of red while waiting for their dinners to arrive. Many of the patrons acknowledged them as they passed by, their respect for the Dean and the surgeon obvious. Davison, the perfect gentleman, gave a brief wave or smile to several women, who tried discreetly to convey their interest in the two men.

"That young Detective Hall is sniffing around again, asking questions," Clark said softly bringing Davison's attention back to him, although his winning smile stayed in place.

"Let him waste his time my friend, he's got nothing." Davison smiled.

"He gave me a hard time, so I rang the Inspector as you suggested."

"Good work. Let the cops chew each other out. It just confuses them more. I hear they think Bella's boyfriends did it anyway." Davison replied snugly.

"There's only one concern I have," Clark confessed. "I saw the nurse, who surprised me near the evidence locker, talking to Hall. It worries me."

"She can't prove anything. She didn't actually see you contaminate the samples, did she?" Davison asked.

"No, no way! But a clever detective might link the contaminated samples to the hospital. That would rule out those two druggies as suspects." Clark concluded. Davison sat for several seconds, lost in thought, his mind looking for a solution.

"She's rather attractive isn't she?" Davison asked smiling.

"Yes, she'd make a great plaything." Clark agreed.

"Maybe our detective is more than interested in just an interview?" Davison suggested.

"You could be right. The detective walked her to her car, then took down her details." Clark informed him.

"Well maybe if you check her schedule, we can see when she's off in the next few weeks. I'd say our friend Detective Hall will ask her out and then we can have our fun." Davison chuckled.

"We could make it look like an accident." Clark put forward thinking of a fitting end for his two problems.

"I was thinking more of a double murder. We can make it look like Bella's friends were involved." Davison replied chuckling.

"Yes. We could then arrange for some evidence to turn up at Bella's friend's farmhouse, which should tie them up very neatly. " Clark smiled.

"Good, tomorrow find her address and get a copy of her shifts, and then we'll see what happens," Davison suggested, as their food arrived.

"Another thing, it might be best to be seen in the company of women. It might allay any suspicions of our private lives." Clark said softly.

"Are you sure? I don't really enjoy their company at all." Davison admitted.

"I know how you feel, but do it anyway. And remember no violence." Clark smiled.

"You're no fun at all, my friend." Davison chuckled, as Clark smiling, poured another glass of wine for each of them.

"Changing the subject, how long till we can have another plaything?" Clark asked hopefully.

"Too risky at the moment I'm afraid, and we do have our night with the detective and his whore coming up." Davison reminded him.

"I was thinking of a visit to one of our favourites?" Clark smiled, trying hard not to maintain his composure.

"Splendid idea. It will give us a release without the complications."

"I was thinking about Julie?" Clark whispered.

"Oh, you are a naughty boy." He sniggered knowing why he'd picked her.

Driving back home alone after finishing his meal, Clark thought over Davison's plan. Finishing off the nosey detective and the nurse and planting evidence at the farm where Bella lived with her friends was a stroke of genius. Added to that was the coming visit to Julie's home, which made him involuntarily lick his lips in anticipation. Unlike Davison who seemed to have the patience of a stone, Clark knew he needed something else to quell his insatiable hunger.

Recalling his visit to Bella in the hospital with his students, he remembered Bella's friend named Kirra. She was strikingly beautiful, the perfect addition to his collection of playthings.

"Maybe I should do a little recon, give Kirra a glimpse of my presence?" He concluded. Chuckling happily to himself, he turned around, driving towards Michael's farm. He knew Davison wanted him to lay low, but what he didn't know wouldn't hurt him Clark figured, laughing merrily to himself.

Family

Bella sat with her friends enjoying the evening. They were just sitting on their veranda, listening to the noises of the night. Bats screeching, cows mooing, and the millions of different insects calling to each other. They sang to her tonight as if she was listening to an orchestra playing. Since the finding of her bike, Bella's mood had lightened, as the truth began to make its way to the surface. She'd made love to Jed last night, needing a release to her pent-up anger.

Like most women raped, she at first loathed being touched by Jed and Michael, preferring Kirra's company at night. Deep down she had missed their company in bed, knowing they weren't to blame. Still, she kept her distance from them, her emotional scars creating a barrier between the boys and herself. Getting high with Kirra had been her attempt to hide the pain. All it had done instead was prolong the misery she felt. Then the in an effort, to break through, the boys had risked everything, to find out the truth.

Seeing their love for her in trying to find out what had occurred that night, had broken through the mental block she had, returning her to their beds. She could see in their eyes how happy they were to have the old Bella back again. Kirra, who had stayed with her every night, abstaining from lovemaking with the boys, had giggled like a young child as Bella went to Jed's bed. She knew the experience had changed her forever, taking away her carefree search for the good in people. Though here with her friends she knew she was safe, and at the moment that was what she craved.

Jed sat on the veranda's front steps feeling vindicated by the finding of the bike. He had at first been unsure of Bella's story, though he always knew that the Dean was behind it somehow. Bella returning to his bed meant everything to him. Without Bella's and Kirra's love, Jed had felt empty, somehow responsible for this whole mess. Their descent into using had rocked him, to the core. It had been the low point in his life, and although he helped them break free, he still felt responsible for the whole situation.

Sitting there quietly, tears came to his eyes as he realised how important his three friends had become to him. Hooked on drugs, knowing life for him was a constant battle to just survive, Jed knew, that without his friends love, he was finished.

Michael lay next to Kirra admiring her body. She had rolled up into a ball next to him, sharing his warmth. She had come to him wanting to share his bed, as Bella shared Jed's. Their lovemaking had been incredibly aggressive as both tried to satisfy their pent-up frustration at being apart. Michael had cried out with Kirra, celebrating their reunion, hugging each other long into the night.

The following day exhausted, they'd stayed in bed only leaving to eat. Now they all sat together on the front veranda, enjoying the evening. Stretching, Kirra stood up yawning, asking if anyone wanted a nightcap before they turned in. Getting their orders for a hot chocolate each, Kirra went to the kitchen preparing their drinks. Humming merrily she dished out the chocolate powder, sugar and milk, while she waited for the water to boil. Glancing out the rear kitchen door, she saw the moon shining brightly in the distance.

"What a perfect." Was all she got out, as a shadow momentarily covered the moon, stopping the light. Scared, Kirra jumped back from the door upending the cups, sending them crashing to the ground. Startled she continued to watch the doorway as if expecting some hideous creature to force its way in.

"Are you okay?" Michael yelled from the veranda, hurrying in.

"Yes, just being clumsy." She replied her fear retreating with Michael's presence.

"Are you sure, you look a little rattled," Michael asked, watching her. Kirra at first thought to tell him of the shadow. Thinking that it could upset Bella and she really didn't see anything anyway, she decided not to worry them.

"No, I'm okay, just been a big day." She smiled as Michael pulled her to him, kissing her. Outside amongst their fruit trees, the shadow moved down the hill, chuckling softly to itself.

The Date

Brett checked his appearance in the mirror for a second time, making sure he looked good. This would be his second date with Wendy, and he wanted it perfect. On his first date with her, he'd taken her out to a well-known local Chinese restaurant, to talk about the case. The case had been forgotten as soon as she came out to his car when he arrived at her unit block. She'd been waiting for him, a good sign he thought as he drove her to the restaurant sneaking little glances at her sensational dress. It was a deep blue colour, which hugged her perfect figure.

Sitting at the lights talking nervously, he stole several looks at her ample cleavage until she informed him the lights had changed, making him go crimson as he drove off. It had been a wonderful night followed by some heavy passionate kisses on her front doorstep. Now on the second date, he hoped to go further, though just the thought of kissing her again drove him nuts. Tonight he'd booked a restaurant at Byron down on the water, knowing he'd have a long drive back to her place. Plenty of time to stop somewhere he smiled as arousal made him adjust his pants and concentrate on driving.

Arriving at her unit this time she wasn't out front, so being a gentleman, he walked to her door rather than honk the horn. Knocking Brett waited expectantly, as after a small wait the door opened. She was still in her nurse's uniform. Telling him to come in, Wendy told him to sit down near the television while she finished getting ready. She'd explained how she'd had a long day and had just arrived home. Brett assured her it was okay, as she hurried off leaving him to look around.

Turning on the TV, Brett took in the room, taking in the photos of her family that covered the walls. He was just about to sit down when he realized he hadn't told her where they were going.

"I've booked a place at Byron tonight. I thought you might like seafood or something." Brett yelled out, over the shower running.

"Sounds great!" she called back, Brett turned towards the noise. The bathroom was at the end of the hallway leading from the room he stood in. Looking down the hallway, he saw the door was partially open giving him a view into the mirror on the opposite wall. Wendy stood with her back towards the mirror washing her hair. It was the most erotic thing he'd ever seen, as he stood spellbound by her.

Unable to look away, he watched the suds run down her back, down between the cheeks of her arse, before sliding down her firm thighs. As if she sensed he was peeking or had picked up on how quiet he was, she turned, looking into the mirror.

"Sorry!" Was all Brett could think to say, as he turned back to the television, hoping he hadn't blown it.

"Brett," Wendy said softly, making him turn. She stood in the bathroom doorway naked. "Why don't you join me?" She whispered, as Brett slowly got up.

"I couldn't help it." He apologised, unable to stop staring at her body, as he walked down the hallway to her.

"It's okay." She whispered, reassuring him.

Coming into his arms, kissing him, she undid his pants letting them drop to the floor. Brett in the meantime hungrily devoured her lips, removing his shirt and then his underwear. Naked they kissed, moving into the shower. He had never had someone wash his hair before. It was so sensual, and he was so aroused, that he thought he explode, right there and then.

Tired of waiting, he lifted her onto him, impaling her. Hearing her moan, he felt her legs come around his waist gripping him, moving on him. It was over quickly, as they dried themselves moving to the bedroom.

"Still want to go out?" She giggled.

"No, I've got everything I want right here." He smiled, as ready again, he passionately kissed her, before pushing her onto the bed entering her again.

Outside Clark and Davison watched from their car. Seeing Brett was staying they drove off.

"Not tonight, but soon we'll get another plaything." Clark smiled.

"It's a dark night, let's not waste it." Davison giggled, starting the car. "Where too?"

"Julie's house."

"Oh goody," Davison answered, as they both laughed.

JULIE'S HOUSE

It had been a long hard shift. Everyone was glad that the paper was complete, ready to go to print for the next day's distribution. Julie yawning slowly rose from her desk stretching. Julie was one of ten journalists producing the local paper. They all enjoyed that moment of satisfaction when the edition was put to bed.

Julie was responsible for the advertising in the paper. The advertising was the lifeblood of the paper, providing the income that paid the bills and their wages. The viability of the local papers was always an issue, and this paper, was in worse shape than some, a fact Julie kept to herself. Around her, unaware of the financial situation, her fellow friends and workers prepared to leave.

The clock showed 1:00am causing a ripple of fear in Julie. Her step quickened as she walked out the door in a sea of fellow workers. 'Goodbyes and see you tomorrow' echoed through the car-park, as Julie rushed to her car. Opening the door, she swiftly checked the back and front seats. Sure the car was empty, she jumped in, locking her door behind her. Safely inside she steadied herself taking several deep breaths before starting her car. This is where it had happened, her subconscious mind screamed. Remembering that night, made her sob involuntarily while trying to hold back tears.

She'd been working a late shift, like tonight. The paper had gone to print, and as usual, she had stayed behind to check over her work. At the time she had been new to the paper and trying to prove herself to the boss. Leaving the office, she had walked briskly to her car through the deserted car-park. She'd never been scared of the dark, being a bit a loner. When away from work, she enjoyed walking; taking solitary strolls into the surrounding hills.

Her reason for hurrying was a couple of weeks ago she'd seen the shadowy outline of a man, watching her from the adjoining factory complex. Despite the fact that nothing had occurred and she hadn't seen the shadow again, it had scared her. She knew it was silly and she'd even laughed with fellow staff members over the incident. Jittery Julie they had nicknamed her, though some warned her about staying late on her own. Undeterred and determined to put it behind her, she'd shrugged off worries, continuing to work late.

Reaching her car, she quickly opened it climbing inside. Locking the door she looked around, seeing nothing out of the ordinary. Relaxing feeling better, she turned on the engine. Putting the car into reverse, she turned around to look behind her car. Instead, she came face to face with a black ski mask. Terror froze her mind and body as a rope slapped down around her throat, pulling tight. Reflecting on events, she realized he must have gained entry to her car earlier in the night and waited patiently for her to return.

Gasping for breath, she grabbed the rope and tried to scream, as she was pulled against the back of her seat. The hooded figure maintaining his grip on the rope, reached over, opening her door. Another hooded figure then appeared from outside her door. The engine being turned off was the last thing she remembered of her kidnapping, as a rag was held over her mouth. It was covered with something vile, which made her gag. Coughing, fighting for breath she felt her strength drain from her, as she fell asleep.

Julie awoke, finding herself naked and tied to a bed, by her hands. Standing watching her were two naked men, their hooded masks still in place.

"Well, well, well. She's finally awake." One man giggled, moving towards her. Pulling at her ropes trying to get free Julie screamed trying to attract someone, anyone to help her. Both men instead of appearing unworried by her screams encouraged her to shout louder, laughing insanely as she continued. In the end, her voice broken by her constant cries for help forced her to stop. She then watched the men silently move towards her one standing next to the bed on each side of her.

"Now it's our turn to make you scream plaything." One of them whispered as they both climbed onto the bed with her.

That had been two years ago. No one was ever caught for her rape and degradation at the hands of those two monsters. Drugs had been found in her system at the time, giving her details a sketchy at best description of what had happened. The police she saw weren't convinced of what really occurred giving her case low priority. After months seeing shrinks, she had returned to work to a wall of silence. Most believed her story, though no one broached the subject, for fear of unbalancing her more than she already was. Although the whole incident was brushed under the carpet, no employee left the paper alone, making sure everyone was safe, and in their own way showing they believed her.

A bang at her window made her jump. It was Helen, her boss. "Don't forget the board meeting tomorrow." She reminded her, moving off to her own car. Signalling an okay, Julie started her engine driving away.

Arriving at her apartment in Ballina, a seaside town south of Byron, she parked her car outside the front door. Looking around seeing no one, she alighted from her car moving quickly to the front entrance. The door had a swipe card entry, so she quickly fumbled her card out, continually watching the street around her. Once inside she relaxed knowing the building was under constant surveillance. That was the reason why she'd bought a unit here after her rape and abduction, to protect her from her demons.

Checking her mailbox, she casually pressed the lift button leafing through her mail. Entering the lift, she again used her swipe card, pressing her floor button at the same time. Her building had one unit per floor giving the building a fort like quality, denying access to anyone other than who the owner wanted there. Alighting on her floor she opened the door to her apartment. Placing her mail on a side table, she moved towards her bedroom, when she noticed a message on her answering service. Deciding to find out who had rung she pressed the voice button.

"Hello plaything, how are you. We're coming for you." The voices musically announced, to a still room. Julie stood like a piece of stone unable to move. There was no doubt in her mind that the voices belonged to her demons. Sobbing uncontrollably, scared to death that they were already in her unit Julie remained frozen, as her mind tried to fight through her fear.

Shaking herself, coming to life, she raced to the door checking the lock. Sure the door was secure she locked the deadbolt as well. Backing away, watching the door as if expecting the door to somehow open of its own accord, she tried to pull herself together. Grabbing a knife from the kitchen, she went room to room checking the entire unit. Sure she was safe she ran to the phone.

"You won't get me again!" she screamed, dialling triple zero, she waited.

"Can I help you?" an efficient voice asked.

"I need help, I need the police!" she screamed into the phone.

"Okay, relax lady. Give me your address, we'll send a police car." The voice assured her. Quickly reeling off her address Julie crying uncontrollably ran to her bedroom, locking the door. For ten minutes she hid until she heard her intercom phone ring. Running to the wall phone, she picked it up.

"Who is it?" she asked.

"It's the police. You called triple zero. Can you let us in?"

"Come up straight away." She cried her relief at their presence overwhelming. Pressing the front of the building entry door button, she let them into the building before pressing her floor button for the lift to work. Opening the front door, she rushed out to the lift her fear of being alone, becoming unbearable. The two police upon exiting the lift were crushed by the woman, who sobbed uncontrollably. Breaking themselves free from her grip, they sat her down, asking what had occurred.

Going from near hysteria to absolute terror she told them what had happened to her and the call. The officers dutifully wrote everything down exchanging glances at the woman's emotional stability. Checking the building assuring her she was safe, they left her after staying for over an hour.

"It's just a prank phone call they assured her. Best to take some tablets and get a good night's sleep," The officers advised, leaving unsure as to what they could do for her. As one last way of reassuring her, they promised to call in again that night and check on her. To Julie it was as if the light went with them, leaving her defenceless, in the dark. Turning on every light in the house, she barricaded the door. Arming herself again with a kitchen knife she rechecked every room and cupboard. Too scared to go to bed she opted to sit in the lounge room, too terrified to sleep.

After an hour of gut-wrenching loneliness, the wall phone's shrill tone erupted, making her jump to her feet. Running to the phone, she softly asked who it was.

"It's the police were just checking on you. Are you okay?" The voice asked her.

"Yes but I'm terrified." She sobbed breaking down pleading for help.

"Look we'll come up for a while, you don't sound good." The Officer suggested.

"Thank you." She practically cried, her sanity restored by the officers returning. Pressing the front entry door release and the lift buttons, she ran to the door removing her barricade of furniture. Checking her appearance making sure she looked presentable, she waited by the lift. 'Once we're inside, I'll make a coffee or something for them, make them stay as long as possible,' she thought, starting to recover from her fright. As the lift light clicked on Julie smiled ready to welcome her protectors. Instead, two men dressed in black wearing hoods emerged.

"Are you surprised to see us plaything! Did you miss us?" They giggled, rushing towards her. Ripping at her clothing, she was forced back inside her unit. Watching the two hooded monsters following her, seeming in no hurry, she tried to think of an escape. Coming up with an idea, she swiftly moved to the door and attempted to slam it shut. It was to no avail the move had been anticipated, the men shoved the door towards her, throwing her backwards.

Scared senseless, knowing her fate, Julie ran out onto the balcony. In a futile gesture, she slammed the balcony door closed behind her, knowing the lock was on the inside. Grabbing a chair she wedge it behind the door, hoping to hold it shut.

"Come back inside plaything, we want to listen to your beautiful screams." One of the men giggled, as Julie held the chair with what was left of her failing strength. Tired of waiting, the two men threw their combined weight against the balcony door.

Whimpering in terror, Julie saw the door slowly edge open.Giving up any chance of holding the door shut, Julie retreated to the balcony handrail, defeated. Trembling uncontrollably she watched the two men walk out onto the balcony and slowly strip off their clothes in front of her.

"Scream for us plaything. We want to hear you scream as we make sweet love too you." One snarled, his voice feral, as splitting up they came at her from two directions. Julie in desperation turned and lunged over the balcony rail, screaming all the way down to the concrete driveway below.

The men caught off guard, ran to their clothes, quickly dressing. Wiping down any surface they may have touched, they left, locking the door behind them. Ten minutes later the police arrived, responding to a call from a neighbour, about the screams. Finding her dead on the street below her balcony, the police called for backup. With the assistance of a neighbour, the police gained entry to the building.

Reaching her floor finding the door locked from the inside, they kicked it in. Seeing no sign of forced entry, the police waited for their local detectives to arrive. When it was found the police had called earlier, the Detectives called in the two officers who were there first, meeting them at the Ballina police station. After giving statements, about the distressed state of the woman, the death was put down as suicide. Her friends and neighbours sadly would accept the coroner's report.

"Well, that was a surprise." Clark smiled, driving back to their home.

"Pity though, I was looking forward to enjoying Julie again. She had the most amazing scream of any of our victims. I would've really liked to have listened to them again." Davison confessed.

"Still in a way it was quite satisfying to see the effect we had on her." Clark pointed out, as Davison sniggered uncontrollably agreeing.

THE PACT

It had been two weeks since the finding of Bella's bike and still no word from the cops, Michael thought as he finished his breakfast. Going to the phone he rang the police station, asking for Detective Hall. Being put on hold, Michael waited. After listening to several boring pieces of music, Detective Hall's voice came through.

"This is Detective Hall. Is that you Michael?" Brett asked.

"Yes, detective I was just wondering what was happening?"

It's slow going, Michael. I won't know anything for a couple of weeks I'm afraid."

"I thought after the bike things would get moving," Michael exclaimed, disappointed.

"Give me time Michael, it's going slow, but it will get there just be patient," Brett answered, before hanging up with a quick goodbye. Michael stood there looking at the phone, wondering if he was getting the runaround. As the others came out for breakfast, Michael told them of the conversation.

"The cops will do nothing Michael. It was a waste of time going there." Jed spat out.

"He seems a pretty decent bloke." Michael retorted.

"Look all we proved was Bella reached their house. It's not enough for them to do anything." Jed concluded.

"I think he's right Michael, we have to do more," Kirra added.

"Like what?" Michael asked.

"We could look around their house," Jed suggested, making the others go silent.

"I can't go near there!" Bella cried out, fear radiating from her.

"Only Michael and I will enter, you and Kirra can keep watch at each of the two entrances," Jed suggested, having already planned for the visit.

"I can't get caught Jed," Michael said softly, as fear gripped him.

"I wouldn't survive inside either my friend, so we have to decide what happens if we're caught," Jed suggested.

"I'd rather be dead, than in jail with my old man," Michael confessed.

"Okay, we'd rather die than be in jail. I'm happy with that!" Jed agreed.

"What are you two suggesting? That we all kill ourselves if the cops try to lock us up!" Bella stammered out, her eyes misting up.

"We're not suggesting anyone do anything. We're just saying that Jed and I can't go to prison, that's all." Michael reiterated, knowing each person must make his or her own decision.

"Then we shouldn't go near their house!" Bella was adamant.

"We have to do something Bella. They might come for you if they think you're a danger to them." Jed pointed out seeing Bella's eyes take on a haunted look, as Michael pulled her to him, holding her.

"You're right Jed, we have to do something, but I'd have to think about the other thing," Kirra whispered unsurely.

"We will all have to think about what happens if we are caught. I couldn't live without you three." Bella sobbed, coming together the four of them hugged each other, leaving the decision to each to decide.

"Look, so far we haven't been caught. So let's plan this visit to the Deans house, so we don't have to make that kind of decision." Michael put forward, being optimistic about the raid.

Once the group of friends had nutted out a plan, they all went to bed. Kirra stayed with Bella wanting to discuss with her what the boys had suggested.

"I'm not sure what to do if we're caught Kirra. I couldn't live without them, but my beliefs forbid me from taking my own life." Bella whispered into the dark room, her heart opened to her friend.

"I too wouldn't want to live without them Bella, they're all I've got. If the choice is waiting for those monsters to come for us, or prison, I'd choose to go to the next life with them." Kirra softly answered. Reaching across Bella pulled her friend to her, hugging her until sleep swept over them.

The next day at 10.30 in the morning, Michael apprehensively, drove his friends past the Deans house. Watching for movement, they continued on down a dead end lane, bordering the Dean's property. Parking in a heavily forested area, they waited silently, while Jed made sure no one was home. Getting the all clear from him, they left the car, walking across a paddock to where Bella's bike had been found.

Bella, white in the face, walked as if expecting at any moment to be confronted by Clark and Davison. The thought of returning here after what had happened to her was pushing her to her mental limits. She knew that the only thing stopping her from running back to the car screaming was her friend's support. Her job luckily kept her away from the house.

Between them, they had two mobile phones. Kirra took one, while Michael had the other. Kirra and Bella's job was to remain hidden down the road, a hundred metres from the entrance. They were to ring the boys if anyone came down the road, then walk away. They'd then all meet back at the car. It was a good plan, as this road led to four dirt roads, which all dead-ended, making this direction the only one someone would approach from.

Jed and Michael, after the girls had taken up position, approached the garage first. The door wasn't locked, and a search revealed nothing but an old brown van. The garage was evidently used for storage only, and was heavy with dust, meaning no one had been in here for some time. The boys disappointed, reluctantly moved on, knowing what they were looking for would be inside the house.

Approaching the back door, Jed tried the handle. It was locked, which came as no surprise. Checking the windows, Jed found one near the kitchen open, so with a hand up from Michael, Jed slipped inside. Several seconds passed by, before the back door swung open and Michael entered. Both searched the bottom floor from top to bottom, finding nothing, not even a spot on the carpet. It became obvious that the carpet was new.

"The whole floor coverings have been replaced, Jed!" Michael snapped, startling Jed.

"Keep it down Michael, just keep looking," Jed suggested scared by his friend's lack of caution. After an hour of time wasting, they moved upstairs searching the bedrooms there. Another hour found the two men sitting on the stairs feeling miserable.

"There's nothing here mate, the whole place is spotless." Jed sighed, admitting defeat.

"Look these sicko bastards went to a lot of trouble to bring these women here. They must have kept some type of record of these nights?" Michael put forward thinking. "Did you see a movie camera or an ordinary camera?"

"No. You're right, I haven't seen anything like that, and in their jobs, you'd think they'd have at least one," Jed replied smiling, knowing Michael was onto something.

"We're not looking in the right spot. There's got to be somewhere else?" Michael mumbled more to himself than Jed, as he looked around. His thoughts were interrupted as the phone rang. Grabbing it, Michael answered it swiftly, as Kirra voice screamed into the phone. "Someone's coming Jed, run for it!" Michael bellowed as they both raced downstairs.

Going out the back door, Jed slammed it behind him locking it, as they both hurdled over the side hedge into the paddock. Here they remained motionless. The vehicle was from the local Post Office, here to deliver a parcel. The driver unaware he was being watched, left the parcel near the rear door. Casually looking around he unzipped his pants, urinating on the garden before driving off.

Once he'd left Jed and Michael relaxing, stood up behind the hedge.

"God I nearly had a heart attack!" Jed laughed, Michael, joining in, relieving the pressure, as the girls came running up to them.

"That was close!" Kirra whispered, out of breath from running. Bella sat down next to Michael, terrified by the encounter, unable to talk. Jed curiously stared at the parcel, wondering what was in it.

"Keep watch I'm going to look at the parcel." He announced, making ready to move to the rear of the house.

"Don't go back Jed, it's too dangerous!" Bella screeched, startling him.

"Why risk it?" Michael asked him.

"Because we've got nothing, I'm not leaving without something to justify the risk."

"Okay, but wait till the girls move back up the road into position," Michael suggested, getting support from the girls.

Five minutes later Jed and Michael examined the parcel. It had an invoice on it, so Jed carefully removed it.

"It's a large pile of blank DVDs for recording," Jed told Michael.

"I didn't see a computer with a burner on it in there, did you?" Michael answered getting a 'no' from Jed.

"Then there's somewhere in there we didn't look mate." Jed put forward, looking again at the house. Walking around the outside of the house this time, both young men searched for something out of the ordinary. Michael spotted what they were looking for first. There were two air vents on the rear side of the house hidden behind shrubs. Lying on the ground Michael and Jed looked into the small ventilation shafts, seeing a brief section of a room underneath the house.

"It's an old bomb shelter! It could've been here since the Second World War!" Jed exclaimed as Michael's phone started to ring again. Answering it, Jed waited nervously beside him.

"Run!" He screamed shoving Jed, showing the urgency. This time when they'd cleared the hedge, they didn't stop. They kept going, meeting the girls at the Ute. The message warned Michael that Clark was coming, it was sent by a petrified Bella.

Breathing heavily the four collapsed next to the car too scared to talk for several minutes.

"That was close Jed. He could've seen us." Bella sobbed, her whole body shaking.

"It was worth it, we know where their hiding place is!" Jed replied, watching the surrounding area.

"What good is that Jed?" Michael asked. "No one's going to search their house on our say so."

"We know about the bunker!" Jed pointed out.

"How did we find out Jed? Do you think the cops will like the fact that we broke in here?" Michael shot back, silencing him.

"We can come back and try again," Jed suggested.

"Let's go home, we can discuss it there," Kirra whispered, ending the argument, worried for Bella. The drive home was eerily silent, no one talked. Drained by the day's events, they all thought over what the trip had achieved. Pulling up at the house, Bella ran inside to the bathroom throwing up. Kirra stayed with her that night comforting her, trying to keep away the demons that threatened her very sanity.

Jed and Michael, abandoned by the women, sat on the veranda looking out over the farm glad to see it again.

"We won't be going back there will we?" Jed asked softly.

"Not the four of us, just us two and not for a while, okay," Michael whispered watching the door.

"We did the right thing didn't we?" Jed asked.

"Yes we did, though knowing something doesn't always help," Michael replied, relaxing in his chair.

"He didn't see us did he?" Jed whispered.

"I wouldn't think so, but tonight just in case, we'll both keep watch," Michael replied as they both stared out into the darkness, uneasy by what could be waiting there.

That same night, Wendy arrived home late after doing an afternoon shift. She had been looking forward to seeing Brett again, but he too was working. Having a quick shower, she thought again of her shower with Brett, hoping she hadn't come on too strong.

She'd deliberately left the bathroom door ajar to tempt him. As she showered, knowing he would be watching, she'd become excited beyond belief, wanting him. Turning around, catching him watching her, she'd heard him apologise, sounding deeply embarrassed. She knew then that the time was right.

"I can't believe I walked out naked, like a whore soliciting a client." She giggled out loud remembering. Why she had done it, she didn't know, but it had worked. Their lovemaking had been intense; so much so that even thinking about it made her touch herself, wishing he was here now.

Looking up at the window, feeling slightly guilty, she saw a shadow flash by it. Jumping up, covering her mouth to stop a scream, she moved back from the window, covering herself. Standing too scared to move, she continued to watch the window, until summoning some courage, she moved forward, looking outside.

There she saw a stray dog, sniffing around the garbage bins. Smiling feeling silly, she checked the windows and doors were locked, before turning off the light and going to bed. Still, whatever it was had frightened her, she realized, taking quite a while to fall asleep. Across the road, Clark sat in his car sniggering before driving off.

THE MORGUE

A week after Michael and Jed had searched Clark and Davison's home, found Detective Johnson and Detective Luke at the Morgue. They both stared at the two charred bodies with a mixture of horror and anger. The two bodies had been found in bushland to the north of Lismore in an area famous for young people making out in cars. Actually, it had been one of these young couples, who had come across the grizzly remains while parking there.

"Any ID found on the two victims?" Johnson asked Ross.

"Yeah, the local boys just did a search of the area. They've found some clothes and belongings scattered about, near where the fire took place. They're bagging it and bringing everything they found back to the station now." Ross informed him.

"Any idea of the cause of death? Other than the obvious." Johnson asked the Coroner.

"The male was shot first through the spine, rather neat really." The Coroner smiled, as he continued to examine the bodies.

"What was neat about it?" Johnson replied gruffly, thinking the Coroner had been doing this job for way too long.

"Whoever shot this fellow, wanted him paralysed, but alive. I'd say he was shot while they tortured the young woman. Most probably wanted him to watch I'd say? It was done with surgical precision, cutting the spinal cord while avoiding major veins and arteries." The Coroner concluded sounding impressed, as both detectives flinched at the cold-blooded murder of this couple.

"Anything else you can tell us?" Johnson asked glad to be leaving.

"Not really, they're both badly burned. It will take me awhile to work out the woman's cause of death, although I'd hazard a guess and say some sort of strangulation by the traces of cord around her neck." The Coroner concluded, as the two detectives feeling slightly nauseous left.

"God! What a way to go?" Luke exclaimed as the two men entered their car.

"Yeah, pretty gruesome, nearly made me puke. Hey how about calling Detective Hall, I'd like to see his reaction to seeing the bodies." Johnson smiled.

"Good idea." Luke chuckled, grabbing his phone. As he dialled Halls mobile, Johnson drove the car back towards the station. After several rings, the phone was picked up, and a voice asked who was calling. Luke started telling Hall, about needing him to look at a body at the morgue. In midsentence, he stopped and went silent, as the colour started to drain from his face.

"What the hell's wrong?" Johnson asked as he watched Luke turn towards him stunned unable to talk. Pulling over, Johnson looked at his partner knowing something bad had happened. He waited patiently for him to say something.

"That was one of the local cops at the spot where the bodies were found. The phone belongs to one of the victims!" Luke stammered out, wiping his eyes to clear the tears that started to cascade down his face.

"God no." was all Johnson could say.

Earlier That Night

Brett was on cloud nine as he again drove over to Wendy's unit. He was hooked and knew he wanted more than just these sexually charged nights. This was his fourth night in a row staying at Wendy's, and tonight he'd decided to broach the subject of her moving in with him. Pulling up across the road his blood racing he hurried to her door knocking with a musical rhythm. The door unlocked swung open with his tapping, so he entered wondering what surprise she had for him tonight.

Calling her name getting no answer, he moved towards the bedroom. Tapping on the door it swung open, standing there smiling, he saw Clark holding a scalpel to Wendy's throat.

"Drop your weapon officer." Clark smiled his eyes wild. Brett knew they both were dead if he did, so pretending to comply; he went for his pistol. He was just about to draw and fire, when a club smashed down against the rear of his head. Collapsing to the floor, Brett's last glimpse was of Wendy falling to the floor as well.

When Wendy had arrived home, she had no idea that Clark and Davison were already there. Having climbed in the rear window, they had laid in wait for her to arrive. Once inside they had swiftly overwhelmed her, tying her up and drugging her. With time to kill, both had raped her, taking turns, while keeping watch for Detective Hall. When he had arrived that night; he'd fallen into the trap all too easily.

Now dark outside, they had bound and drugged them both, before putting them into the rear seat of Wendy's car. Clark had then driven her car, while Davison followed in his. Arriving at the secluded off road location, they'd dragged Hall out, tying him to a tree opposite the car. As the drug wore off, Brett through bleary eyes saw Wendy spread-eagled on her car bonnet. The shock of seeing what was going on made the effects of the drug dissipate rapidly. Brett threw everything he had into breaking loose. Clark and Davison seeing him struggling walked over smiling.

"How's our inquisitive detective. Feeling clever now are we?" Clark asked as Davison chuckled. Brett made to answer, when Clark placed his own gun against his stomach, pulling the trigger. Behind them, Wendy screamed behind her gag trying to help. Groaning overwhelmed with pain, Brett cursed them, spitting in Clark's face. He in turn slowly wiped his face with his sleeve grinning.

"You won't die yet detective, not till we're finished with your girlfriend." Clark sniggered as the two men moved back to the car and Wendy. Both again raped her letting Brett watch, as his life slowly drained from him. Releasing Wendy's gag, they let her scream into the night, laughing hysterically as their plaything struggled for life. Finished they placed a rope around her neck, pulling it tight.

"Are you happy now detective?" Davison asked, only to find Brett's lifeless eyes staring back at him. "Pity I would've liked him to see her last moments.' Clark giggled, before going to their car and retrieving a drum of petrol. Dowsing both of them and the car, he lit a match, throwing it from a distance. With a loud thud, the vehicle burst into flames, as Clark and Davison drove away.

"Have you got his badge and gun?" Clark asked.

"Yes, we'll drop them tomorrow night at Bella's farm."

"What a night." Clark smiled.

Soul Searching

When it was found that one of the victims was a detective, all hell broke loose. The Superintendent ordered a task force be set up immediately. It wasn't long before the identity of the woman was found to be Nurse Black. Detective Johnson and Detective Luke sat in their office silently watching the station fill with detectives from Sydney. One look at their faces told you everything. Because of their close relationship with Detective Hall, they'd been excluded from the investigation. The Superintendent had told them angrily to back off after Johnson blew his stack at being left out. Now they sat doing nothing, while outsiders looked into the murder.

"Well, that's, that Dave. I'm sure they'll get the ones responsible." Ross said flatly, trying to get some reaction from his partner.

"Bullshit it is! I'm not sitting here waiting for some blow-ins from Sydney, to prance around here while we make coffee!"

"What about the Super? He'll be pissed if he finds out we're digging into the case.

"Fuck him! Hall and I mightn't have seen eye to eye on much, but he was one of ours. Whoever did this is gonna pay!" Dave spat out.

"Where do we start?" Ross replied, knowing arguing with Johnson was futile.

"If the Sydney mob hasn't got them, grab his case files," Dave ordered, thinking about their next move, as Ross left.

It took Detective Luke several hours to gain the files without being spotted. Sneaking into Hall's office, he grabbed them unnoticed. Walking out he ran into one of the detectives from Sydney. Covering over why he was there, he engaged him in conversation asking how it was going. To his surprise, he found him pretty talkative about the case, and he spotted a glaring mistake in their investigation.

Meeting Dave at the pub that afternoon, they went over Hall's files, in the privacy of a back room the hotelier had let them use.

"And they're not checking his case files?" Johnson asked surprised.

"Yeah, I was surprised too. Seems they think that because he was newly promoted to detective, it's not much point. They believe Hall could have stumbled onto a drug deal or something while out with the nurse." Luke informed him.

"Let them chase that line. Let's concentrate on what he was looking into." Johnson smiled, thinking they could now investigate without crossing the Sydney D's. It took them over two hours to go through Hall's files. He'd been busy; completing 20 cases since making detective. Only one of them was a major case though, and that was still running.

"It keeps coming back to that druggie Bella's rape case doesn't it?" Luke put forward.

"Yeah your right mate, I just don't see those two dimwits doing this, can you?" Johnson answered sounding unsure. He'd been convinced Jed and Michael had attacked Bella. Following Hall's death, doubts started to creep into his thinking.

"In his report, he mentioned a nurse had seen something. Is this the same nurse?" Luke asked fishing. Johnson, without answering looked again at the file, before replying.

"Yes, it is. That ties them both to the case!" Johnson mumbled, deep in thought, wondering if all along Hall had been right.

"You know the other day when you had it out with him, and he reeled off that evidence against Dr Clark and the Dean? Well, I believed him." Luke admitted, not wanting to go against Johnson.

"Yeah, then there's what Creepy at the morgue said about the way Hall was shot. As if the killer knew exactly where his spine was! Those two dope heads wouldn't have the faintest, but a Doctor would."

"You think they did this to cover their tracks!" Luke whispered.

"Yeah, I do my friend. And my stupidity got poor Detective Hall killed."

"It wasn't your fault Dave. Like you said Dr Clark and Davison can have any woman they want, they're loaded."

"That's the problem. I was so convinced that those two low lifes did it, that I didn't ask the obvious question. Why doesn't either of them have a girlfriend?"

MICHAEL'S FARM

The morning after the gruesome discovery, found Kirra making breakfast. Her merriment at listening to the local radio station's music halted when the radio squawked out the news about the murder. Kirra put her hand in her mouth to stop herself from screaming. Running to Michael who was out checking the vegetables, she burst into tears, as Bella and Jed appeared from the house. One look at Kirra made them rush out. Kirra told them what she'd heard as they all guiltily wondered if it was connected to their visiting Davison's farm.

"Look it's got nothing to do with our visit," Jed told them confidently. "If they knew we'd been there they'd have come after us!" he continued. Bella immediately started sobbing hysterically, followed by Kirra, as Jed realised he'd said the wrong thing.

"They're not going to come here stop worrying." Michael told them flatly, giving Jed the 'you're an idiot look' for saying it.

"Maybe we should take some precautions," Kirra suggested nervously.

"If you're really worried, we'll lock the house up at night and there's something else," Michael replied sheepishly. Going back into the house, Michael went to the kitchen. Reaching up on top of a high shelf he pulled down a bag he'd kept hidden there. Pulling out his dad's double-barrelled shotgun, he loaded a shell, into each barrel.

"It belonged to my old man, he used it to rob banks with it. All you have to do is point it and pull one of the two triggers, that should be enough." Michael smiled.

"We'll never reach it up there." Bella pointed out. She was scared of guns, but the alternative to her of falling into Davison's or Clark's hands again was far worse. Looking around Jed offered a solution.

"How about placing it in the kitchen garbage bin? That way you can always grab it in an emergency, and it's safe from being accidentally dropped in there." he smiled.

"Okay, but I don't like guns, and I'm not sure I could shoot someone anyway," Kirra confessed, as the group moving on, sat down to have breakfast.

As Jed and Bella lay naked in Jed's bed that night, Jed thought about poor Detective Hall. He'd believed the cops would do nothing, that's why he had insisted on going to Davison's house. That could've been them burnt to death if those two psychos had of caught them. 'God, maybe they found where we forced the window?' Jed surmised as he lay there sweating.

Climbing out of bed, he moved out onto the deck. Lying down on their old lounge he thought about their situation, giving returning to Davison's house some serious thought. It wasn't long before the first mosquito turned up, followed closely by another. Getting up, not wanting to disturb Bella, he grabbed some mosquito netting. Throwing it over the lounge, he then climbed underneath the net, safe from the insects. He lay there silently thinking about his life, and feeling the need, he popped a couple of tablets in his mouth.

Relaxing, he lay there as a feeling of serenity flowed through him. Just about asleep Jed stared out over the property, as a shadow passed by him. At first, he thought he imagined it, having dropped some pills. Lying there he knew he was nearly invisible under the netting, as the shadow of a man again passed by. This time it stopped near the side of the house to his left. The shadow seemed to hesitate as if sensing him before it disappeared under the veranda.

He was just about to get up, when a second shadow passed him, standing above where the first had vanished. Seconds later two shadows stood together looking towards him as real fear gripped him. Too scared to yell out, he lay motionless, expecting at any moment to be dowsed in petrol and set alight, sharing Detective Hall's fate.

Looking again he saw the shadows move away disappearing into the dark night, vanishing like demons. He would never know how long he lay there. Too petrified to move, all he knew was at some stage he must've passed out, not waking till the morning.

As the first rays of sunlight hit the porch, Jed opening his eyes relived his nightmare. Springing to his feet, he fled inside, as if the devil himself was after him. Running blindly, through the house entirely out of control, he tripped over the dining table, crashing to the floor. So frightened was he, that in terror he screamed out, waking the others, as he crawled towards his room.

Bella was first to him, hugging him on the floor as he sobbed in fear.

"What the hell's going on Jed?" Michael yelled, trying to find out what had occurred.

"Shadows, shadows outside, I thought they were going to kill me!" Jed screamed, as his friends seeing the pills that had spilt on the floor, carried him to his room.

Waking up at lunchtime, Jed with an almighty headache stumbled out of bed. Ambling to the kitchen, he opened the first aid kit. Putting two painkillers into his mouth, he washed it down with water, before walking out onto the front veranda. Kirra and Bella sat together as Michael sat opposite, all looked worried.

"Are you okay?" Michael asked, rushing to Jed walking him to a chair, which he crashed down into.

"Yeah, I was pretty spooked. Sorry if I scared you all,"

"What happened? You were screaming like a madman." Bella asked close to tears.

"It was so real. I took two tablets then a shadow appeared and then another. I thought demons were coming for me." Jed admitted clearly upset.

"Has that occurred before?" Kirra asked.

"No, thank God, it's the first time," Jed informed them.

"Where'd you see them?" Bella asked getting up.

"Over there, to the left. One disappeared under the house, the other stood next to it and then they both disappeared." Jed replied, realising how stupid it sounded. Walking over to where Jed had indicated, Bella looked under the house.

"What are you doing Bella?" Michael asked.

"Remember how no one believed me. I just thought I'd check it out. As Jed said, it hasn't happened to him before." Bella answered before suddenly standing up. "Michael! There's something under there in a black plastic bag." She gasped, sounding scared, as Michael rushed over. Climbing underneath Michael grabbed the bag before crawling back out. Standing with the others, he emptied the bag out onto their small coffee table on the veranda. Inside was a pistol and Detective Hall's policemen's badge.

"They're trying to frame us!" Jed exclaimed, sounding both angry and scared.

"What do we do?" Bella asked her eyes red.

"We've got to do something. They could've already rung the cops!" Michael spat out.

"Call them first it's our only chance," Kirra begged, scared to death that these monsters had come to their home.

"They won't believe us!" Jed replied.

"Well, they won't if they come here and we do nothing," Bella replied walking to the phone.

"Let me do it, Bella. You've been through enough" Jed ordered, taking the phone from Bella, as the others gather around him giving support.

Johnson sat stone-faced at his desk trying to work out what to do first. Hall had two leads running, the Forensic report and the missing girl. The girl search could take months, so Johnson thought he'd go with the Forensic department in Sydney. He'd already rung there trying to get the report prioritised. Getting a flat no for his trouble, he now sat brooding wanting to hurt someone. He was interrupted from his dark thoughts by the phone ringing.

"Who is it?" Johnson snarled, crushing his phone with pent-up rage.

"Detective Johnson this is Jed, Bella's friend. Is this a good time to talk?" Jed's voice asked sounding scared. 'Fuck this is all I need, this dickhead ringing me,' Johnson thought sitting there silently.

"Are you there Detective?" Jed asked clearly scared. It suddenly occurred to Johnson that he was scared shitless of him, so why was he ringing?

"No it's not a good time Jed, but what do you want?" Johnson asked civilly.

"It's about Detective Hall's murder." Jed squeaked out.

"Say no more Jed, I'm on the way," Johnson replied excitedly, dropping everything and heading for the door. Spotting Detective Luke down the hall, he pointed to the car smiling, as Luke dropped his coffee in the sink hurrying after him. Jumping into Dave's unmarked police car, Ross waited for the news.

"Jed that druggy friend of Bella's just rung. Wants to see us urgently about Hall's murder." Johnson whispered as if the Superintendent was listening.

"Shit it must be important, he hates our guts!" Ross admitted, remembering the belting they'd given him and Michael.

"That's what I figured. It took guts to ring me. I want to know what he's got!" Johnson replied, hitting the gas.

When they arrived at the farmhouse, an awkward silence settled over the two detectives, Bella and her friends.

"Jed I know we're not friends and there's a good chance we never will be. We want the bastards who killed Hall and that nurse. You want the mongrels that attacked Bella. We both now suspect the same two men, what have you got?" Dave asked.

At first, Jed seemed scared to say anything, a touch from Bella made him start.

"Would you like to sit down with us on the veranda Detectives. It's going to take a while to explain." Jed stammered out, as the two detectives relaxing slightly, sat down. While the girls went to get some drinks, Jed seeing no other way, handed Johnson the bag. Johnson took one look and handed it to Luke.

"Where'd do you find it?" Johnson asked softly, knowing they weren't involved or they wouldn't have given him the gun.

"Two men last night put it under the front veranda. I suppose you'll be getting an anonymous call soon, telling you where to look." Jed said smiling briefly.

"You couldn't tell who they were?" Luke asked

"No. I was a bit stoned. Only saw the shadows while I lay under a mosquito net here on the veranda, or I'd say I'd be dead too." Jed admitted.

"You're right Jed. These two guys have really crossed over, killing you all would mean nothing to these two now." Luke replied, letting the stoned part slide.

"Look this is good, but it leads nowhere. I know you were snooping around with Detective Hall have you got anything more?" Johnson asked sounding desperate.

"We went to Davison's house a couple of days ago," Michael confessed stopping to look at Jed, who nodded for him to continue. "Went through their house, it was clean, so we were about to leave when we realised they didn't have a computer or camera or anything. We looked around outside the house and found some hidden vents. When you look into them, you can see a room under the house." Michael told them realising if they turned on him he'd be in jail for a long, long time.

"Shit you took a chance!" Johnson told them, meaning it in more ways than one.

"This is good, but it won't get us in the front door with a warrant," Luke said, bursting their bubble.

"Yeah, but we're closer! And remember we still got Hall's leads to follow." Johnson answered as the girls appeared carrying drinks.

The group had just started to relax when several police cars came down the road driving up Michael's farm's entrance. Jed at first thought they'd been set up, jumping to his feet looking at Johnson.

"Everybody relax. Let me do the talking," Johnson ordered, as he walked towards his car, casually dropping the bag and its contents on the floor of the rear seat. With a flurry of badges, the Sydney task force arrived at the house.

"What's going on?" Johnson barked, seeing the surprised looks on the city detective's faces.

"We've had a report of shooting out here, and someone reported seeing someone here throw a gun under the veranda." Jones, the lead detective, explained, watching Johnson closely.

"Well go ahead and search. Some smartarse probably saw us drive up here earlier this morning. Thought he'd cause some trouble I'd say?" Johnson replied smoothly.

"Your boss told you two to keep away from Detective Hall's case didn't he?" Jones spat out.

"That's right Detective he did. This is another unsolved case we're working on, so do your search and piss off." Luke growled surprising Johnson.

"We're just doing our job detective remember that," Jones replied visibly backing away from Luke.

The search proved a waste of time as the task force giving Luke and Johnson one last glare, disappeared in a cloud of dust. Once the task force had gone, Johnson and Luke shaking sat down, gulping down Kirra's and Bella's cold drinks.

"Shit that was close!" Luke said smiling.

"God I nearly died when you told that prick to piss off," Johnson confessed chuckling. Turning at the silence, they saw Michael and Jed standing there open-mouthed. "Well if you had any doubts about us Jed they must be gone by now," Johnson admitted, seeing the look of understanding on their faces.

"You're not supposed to be investigating the murder, are you?" Michael asked smiling.

"That's right, so we're all in this mess together." Luke put forward as the group went quiet, remembering why they were all here.

"Do you think you can catch them?" Bella asked, fear in her voice.

"Look one way or another we'll get them. You four keep your heads down; those Sydney detectives will be back for sure, so say nothing. We've got two strong leads that should get us a search warrant for their house. I'm not going to kid you, it's going to take awhile, so sit tight and no more heroics." Dave ordered, getting nods from the four of them. Getting into the car, Dave was just about to drive away when he stopped and got back out.

"Another thing, I'm sorry the way you were all treated, especially you two," Dave said, looking at Jed and Michael, clearly not used to apologising. "I just thought you'd done it that's all," Dave confessed hopping back into the car.

"We'll say we're even when you get those two," Michael replied a slight smile on his face, as the detectives drove away. Looking back in his rear vision mirror, Dave saw Bella and Kirra move over and stand beside Jed and Michael, holding them.

"I was dead wrong about those four!" Dave admitted out loud.

"Yeah, they're weird, but there's something family about them, isn't there?" Ross replied.

"Shit I think we're getting soft!" Dave smiled.

"That'll be the day," Ross answered as both detectives hurried back to the station.

Arriving, Dave and Ross found a reception committee waiting for them.

"You two detectives in here!" the Inspector roared from his office, as Dave and Ross walked by. Entering, they found the four Sydney detectives in there as well.

"Detective Jones here thinks you're interfering with his investigation." the Inspector growled.

"He's full of shit Sir. We went there, following up on a case Detective Hall hadn't closed." Dave replied innocently.

"Why were you there Jones?" the Inspector asked.

"A passing driver reported seeing someone with a gun, throw it under the veranda," Jones replied flatly.

"That's bullshit Sir? The house is a kilometre from the road." Dave tossed in, seeing Jones squirm.

"Who called in the sighting?" the Inspector asked abruptly.

"It was anonymous Sir. But after checking Hall's files, we saw a connection." Jones replied confidently.

"What connection? And why are you only now going through his files? I thought that's where you'd have started." The Inspector barked, making Jones and the other Sydney detectives wince.

"Our investigation went in a different direction. We're rechecking this one just in case." Jones answered smoothly.

"I don't care which fucking direction your case is taking detective! You'd better get the lead out! Is that understood?" The Inspector bellowed, making all the Sydney detectives look at the floor. "And another thing, leave my detectives to investigate the rape case, they at least know what they're doing." The Inspector screamed, leaving his office. The room went quiet with the Inspector's departure, no one knowing what to say.

"You boys have a nice day!" Ross smiled, turning with Dave and leaving.

"Fuck you!" echoed from the room, as outside both men laughed. The Inspector coming towards them made them stop abruptly.

"Both of you outside now." He ordered pointing at the door. The two detectives having no choice silently followed. Once outside, the Inspector after a quick look around continued. "Have you got anything?" He asked softly.

"About what Sir?" Ross answered, acting dumb.

"Don't bullshit me. Have you got a lead on Detective Hall's killers?" The Inspector growled.

"We're pretty sure it was Davison and Clark Sir," Dave confessed he too looked around.

"You're kidding! I thought you said Brett was full of shit when he went after them." The Inspector answered shocked.

"Hall told us, Nurse Black had seen Clark near the evidence locker. At first, I thought it was flimsy, now both the investigating detective and the witness are dead. It's too much of a coincidence, and let's face it, that was the only major case he was working on." Dave admitted sadly. At first, the Inspector seemed unconvinced. Both Clark and Davison had powerful friends and were respected throughout the community. On the other hand two detectives, who both thought they were innocent, now stood before him unafraid to say they were wrong.

"If these two bastards did it I want them taken care of. But make sure you're both dead sure, am I understood!" The inspector said looking around cautiously. "There's another thing. My wife's sister called us last night to tell us Doctor Clark asked her out." The inspector added sounding worried.

"They're covering their tracks, Sir. Taking her out shows their normal and allays any suspicion about their lack of female company." Ross suggested.

"Do you think I should warn her off?" The Inspector asked.

"No, she'll be safe for now, although I'd suggest a public venue. You can say it's so she's seen with him by her friends." Dave put forward, getting the nod from the Inspector.

"Another thing Sir, ring her and asked how it went later that night, we might gain something from his behaviour." Ross smiled, as the Inspector again stood thinking for a while before answering.

"Okay, this stays between the three of us. Keep away from those idiots from Sydney, let them proceed, as they like. You two get Hall's killers!" the Inspector ordered walking back inside.

"What now?" Ross asked Dave softly.

"I'm going to Sydney for a break." Dave smiled.

"You're kidding."

"While I'm there I'll drop around and see an old friend in the Forensic department, I haven't seen old Jim Maloney for years.

"I remember him, he was a detective here when I first arrived here wasn't he?"

"Yes, he was. Unfortunately, he had to leave suddenly for some unknown reason." Dave smiled.

SYDNEY FORENSIC DEPARTMENT

Dave's wife was impressed and slightly suspicious when he offered to take her to Sydney for a few days. Informing the Inspector that he needed a few days off to fix a problem in Sydney, he was immediately given leave. After booking a flight for the following day, Dave went to his small office in the garage at his house. Moving an old filing cabinet, Dave looked around nervously, before unlocking an old safe hidden in the wall. Pulling out a large bunch of old files, he quickly went through them, finding what he needed.

In the police force, Dave had learnt for the sake of his career, to always keep evidence on cases where a crime was committed by a fellow officer and dropped. In most cases, they lacked the evidence to prosecute these men, or sometimes for the good of the force they were let go with a warning. The file he now held was one of these. Closing the safe, Dave quickly moved the filing cabinet back into place, carrying the file up to his room and packing it in his suitcase. Smiling he proceeded to help his wife finish getting ready for their trip the next day.

Arriving in Sydney just before lunch, Helen was shocked to find he'd booked an expensive hotel. It was across from the Opera House in the Rocks area, right on the water.

"God, this must've cost a packet?" She laughed, wondering what her husband was up to.

"Nothing's too good for you darling. I thought tomorrow we could do some shopping then we could go out and see a show. How's that sound?" Dave smiled.

"It sounds a little too good to be true. What's going on Dave?" Helen asked bluntly, her eyes drilling into him.

"Can't a guy take his wife away for a couple of days and pamper her?" Dave answered looking hurt.

"Sure he can, but I know you, Dave, you wouldn't walk away from a murder case, not when it's one of your own men," Helen replied flatly, seeing his eyes start to mist up.

"I know who killed Detective Hall honey, I just can't prove it! I've come down here on the sly to visit the Forensic lab and give them a little hurry up." Dave admitted looking dejected sitting down. His wife, seeing his depressed state came across to him and hugged him.

"Then go get them, tiger, just don't lie to me." She whispered.

"Sorry about that honey, I'll go there straight away. You can do a bit of shopping this afternoon while I'm gone." Dave suggested happily standing up to leave.

"That's a great idea tiger, although it's going to cost you for lying to me." Helen laughed, as she went into the bedroom to change, taking the smile off Dave's face.

The Forensic laboratory was located behind the Police Department's main building in the inner city suburb of Redfern. Saving time Dave opted for a taxi, rather than go by train. Giving the address the driver gave Dave the once over, before driving off as if the Prime Minister was in the vehicle.

"I judge you're a cop?" The driver asked, giving his best smile.

"Yeah, I'm from up north, just visiting a friend who works here," Dave replied, watching the driver relax.

"Where from?" The driver inquired.

"Lismore, it's inland from Byron Bay," Dave answered. Actually, it was a bit south of Byron and quite a drive to Lismore, but most people down south thought everything up north was next to Byron Bay.

"That's where the copper was murdered, wasn't it? I heard some of our detectives have gone up there to help you guys out" The driver replied having heard it on the radio.

"Yeah, they've been a real big help," Dave smiled, as the driver continued talking merrily about anything.

Arriving at his destination, Dave gave the driver a tip, getting a goodbye from him as if they were close friends now. Smiling Dave walked into the front reception area finding a receptionist and a guard in the foyer. Showing his badge, Dave asked to speak to Jim Maloney the head of the Forensic Department.

"Have you an appointment?" The female receptionist asked as the guard looked on.

"No, I haven't. Tell him Detective Dave Johnson is here from Lismore to see him." Dave replied bluntly.

"He's a very busy man Detective." She replied with a bored voice, as the guard smiled at him.

"Do your job and call him now!" Dave ordered, watching both the guard and the girl bristle at his tone. The receptionist at first tried to stare him down, as the guard took on a more menacing stance. It didn't take long for the girl to cave in, picking up the phone and dialling Maloney. Whispering so Dave couldn't hear, a small smile appeared on her face as she lowered the phone.

"Mr Maloney said to tell you, that if you're here trying to hurry the test on the Detective Hall case you're going to be out of a job!" The receptionist replied smiling, giving him a 'you're an arsehole' look as the guard moved in behind him threateningly.

"No, I'm here to interview him about the porn video he made with an underage girl in Byron several years ago," Dave informed her, as the receptionist lost her smile. The guard hearing this and not wanting to be involved promptly left, leaving the receptionist sitting there isolated. "Where's his office?" Dave asked.

"Down the hallway, four doors on the right." The girl informed him, as he started down the corridor, ignoring her. Reaching the door, tapping once, Dave entered to see Jim Maloney about to explode.

"You're finished you arsehole. I'll see you sacked for this. I was cleared of that bullshit charge years ago!" Jim yelled. Dave unaffected by his rage, walked to his little kitchenette, making himself a coffee. "Yeah, just make yourself at home you loser. One call and your shovelling shit for a job." Jim continued, seething with anger.

Still ignoring him, Dave walked over to a DVD player, inserting a disk before turning on the TV screen. In brilliant colour Jim watched himself screwing a very young girl, slapping her several times laughing, as he sniffed what looked like cocaine.

"Could've been a big hit, if you'd had a bigger dick?" Dave chuckled, as Jim sat there frozen.

"That's impossible, I destroyed the disc!" Jim cried out, rushing over to the player. Grabbing out the disk, he smashed it into little pieces, glaring at Johnson.

"The recorder had a memory database built in. I made a couple of copies just in case." Dave admitted, sitting down and drinking his coffee.

"It was a long time ago Dave, I was stupid, give me a break," Jim begged, close to tears.

"I'm not here to arrest you, Jim. I just want you to treat Detective Hall's case with the priority it deserves." Dave replied.

"It's only a test for tampering. That's got no priority here." Jim confessed knowing politics decided which cases received special treatment.

"Bump it up, Jim. He was a cop. I want his killer taken care of. You were a good cop once; try to remember what it's like out there." Dave reminded him, walking to the door.

"Consider it done Dave. But how do I know you won't squeal on me?" Maloney replied flatly.

"Because you're the best Forensic chief this department has ever had. What you did back then is done. Just keep doing your job and remember the cops out there, and this DVD will remain hidden." Dave assured him, as he closed the door behind him.

Walking out past the quiet receptionist, Dave told her to have a good day, not waiting for a reply. Catching a cab back to the hotel, Dave found his wife happily sorting through packages from her afternoon out shopping alone.

"I told you it would cost you." She smiled trying on a new dress. "You better hurry and shower honey; I've booked a very nice restaurant on the harbour for dinner." She giggled.

Smiling, seeing his wife had enjoyed herself, he walked into the bathroom to shower. He didn't care how much this trip cost him. He got what he wanted.

Landing back at Lismore Airport, Dave found Ross waiting for them.

"Thought I'd save you a cab fare?" Ross explained as he helped put their bags in the boot, before driving them home.

"Good trip?" Ross asked.

"I'll say, I think we both got what we went for." Dave's wife laughed, as he joined in, surprising Ross.

"It's a long story Ross, I'll tell you after we get home," Dave replied, chuckling softly.

"You're a lucky man Dave. Most wives promised a romantic couple of days away, mightn't have handled being used." Ross smiled, as he joined Dave in a beer on his back veranda.

"Yeah it cost me, but Maloney speeding up the investigation into the samples, we should have it in the next few days.

"What now?" Ross asked softly, knowing Dave's wife didn't like them bringing their work home.

"We wait for the report and try to find that girl. It's all we've got I'm afraid." Dave confessed as they sat there silently thinking.

THE BIG BREAK

Four days passed before the report from Forensics arrived. Dave at first hesitated when opening the letter fearing it might lead nowhere. Ross, in the end, grabbed the letter ripping the seal, as they both read the report.

"He was right Dave! The samples were deliberately tampered with!" Ross smiled as the trap closed in on Davison and Clark.

"It's still not enough my friend, we need that girl," Dave stated angrily.

"We're on the right track though?" Ross replied cheering his friend up.

"Yes we're a lot closer, the problem is, do we tell the Sydney detectives?" Dave answered.

"It doesn't tell them anything solid. I say we wait till we've found the girl." Ross suggested. Dave was just about to agree when he saw another letter in his pile disregarded when they saw the letter from the Forensic Department.

"Holy Shit!" Dave shouted, seeing the letter marked Department of Mental Health. Tearing it open he read the letter, stating a girl in their Caloundra psychiatric facility to the north of Brisbane was the young woman they were looking for.

"Let's go see the boss and arrange to visit her," Dave suggested, moving towards the door before Ross could answer. Their boss sat silently as his two senior detectives erupted with information.

"Slow down for God's sake!" the Inspector shouted, seeing the excitement in their eyes. "Okay now what have you got?" he continued, pointing to Dave. Dave quickly went over the sample from forensics and the finding of the girl. He also wanted to know if he wanted the Sydney Detectives involved, before waiting for their boss to answer.

"You know my sister-in-law went out with Clark the other night. Said he was a perfect gentleman until she invited him to her unit for the night. He got rough during sex, slapping her several times, even biting her. She told him to leave, and he did, even apologized to her, but he scared her badly." The Inspector said distantly, upset by this information.

"I'm sorry Sir I didn't think he'd get rough," Ross admitted softly.

"Forget it, men, I thought he was innocent, now this. Go see the girl if she backs up the evidence I want them gone, permanently. Is that understood?" the Inspector ordered.

"We'll get em, Sir, you can count on that. Until then I suggest putting them under observation, just in case." Dave suggested, getting immediate agreement from the Inspector.

"What about the Sydney detectives, Boss?" Ross asked.

"I'll tell them that you've found the girl. They can watch the house till you return. Now get going!" He replied as his two men hurriedly left.

It wasn't as simple as they thought, having to first get permission to see the girl. Her doctor seemed bent on giving them a hard time, as Dave informed him they were coming tomorrow if he liked it or not. Slamming the phone down, the two men went home packing for one night.

The next day, at daybreak, they started out. Ross drove, wondering if the doctor could be right that they might be wasting their time.

"What do you think Dave, the shrink seemed convinced she wouldn't answer questions?" Ross asked breaking the silence.

"We'll see when we get there Ross. I'm not letting this go on the word of some smartarse on the end of a phone!" Dave secretly was worried.

Ten sharp that morning Dave and Ross fronted up to the mental wing of the Department of Health facility at Caloundra. Going first to reception, they were escorted by a white-clad guard to Doctor Chamber's office. Standing with the guard, they stood there for ten minutes while the good doctor finished some important forms he was working on.

The guard sensing the tension building, excused himself, leaving the two detectives standing there fuming. Ross having had enough of waiting reached across the desk grabbing the doctor's paperwork. Walking to the window, he opened it, throwing the paperwork out.

"How dare you." The Doctor started, only to be grabbed around the neck by Dave and pulled out of his chair.

"Who'd the fuck do you think you're playing with arsehole?" Dave exploded, as the doctor tried to breathe through his constricting neck. Throwing him back into his chair, Ross took up position to his side while Dave stood over him. "That girl holds a secret to who killed one of our men!" Dave exploded. "Get up off your arse and lead the way to her now," Dave shouted pointing to the door.

The doctor furious at his treatment was about to threaten them with having their badges. Looking at the detective's faces, he realised how over the edge these two cops were. He knew from experience, how dangerous people over the edge could be, from working here. He decided to follow the safest path and comply with their request.

"Okay I'll take you there, there's no need to be so rough." The doctor stammered out. "I've got to warn you though; she hasn't talked for over a year." He added softly trying to placate them. Calling another orderly dressed in white, the doctor instructed him to take them to the patient and assist them. Knowing the patient well, the doctor decided to not be there when they failed to get what they wanted.

Following the silent orderly, Dave suppressed his anger, knowing he'd gone too far with the doctor. He knew he was on edge, knowing that everything hung on some nutcase, locked up for over a year. Rounding a corner, they came to a steel door, where another guard watched the patients through a barred window.

"Everything quiet in there?" Their escort asked the guard at the gate.

"Yeah, it's okay. They shouldn't bother you unless one of you breathes." The Guard laughed. Seeing the two visitors standing like stone watching him, the guard lost his smile quickly, opening the door. Their escort, sensing the anger the two cops projected, handed them on to yet another white-clad orderly, for their final walk down a dimly lit corridor, to Eva's room.

Entering a small room containing just a bed and an opened wardrobe, the two men waited, while the guard went and found the girl. Eva, from the photo given to Detective Hall by her parents, was a happy, full figured girl, with long brown wavy hair. She projected the look of a girl going somewhere, looking forward to the future. Moments later the guard entered leading a wafer-thin girl. Devoid of any emotion, she looked nothing like the picture Dave had seen.

Dressed in a plain blue hospital gown, her head shaved, wearing no makeup, she shuffled past the two detectives before lying down on her bed. Lying there she looked up at the three men through eyes filled with unimaginable fear, before rolling up into the foetal position.

"Eva, my name's Detective Johnson, you can call me Dave. I'd like to ask you a few questions." Dave whispered getting down on one knee beside her. There was no response from Eva, just the same vacant scared look. "It's important Eva, other girls have been hurt. Some have died, we need your help." Dave practically begged as she lay there as if she too was long gone from this earth.

"Waste of time my friend she's a fucking zombie. You may as well talk to the fucking wall; you'll get the same answers. The only thing she's good for is a blowjob once in a while!" The guard laughed, enjoying watching the two cops waste their time. Ross turning swiftly punched the guard in the stomach. Bent over in pain, the guard looked at Ross in shock, as he kicked him in the shins. Landing heavily on the floor, Ross proceeded to drag him out into the hallway. The guard scared, pushed his emergency button, summoning other guards, plus the doctor.

"You've got no right to come in here bashing who you like. I want you both out of here now!" The Doctor screamed, having gained some courage by the presence of four guards. Ross faced them in the hallway, while Dave continued to sit near the girl. "I said for you two to go!" the Doctor repeated, as Ross adjusted his coat showing his gun. The move though casual, made the four unarmed guards look to their doctor. This caused a stalemate as the doctor weighed his options.

In the cell Dave knew Ross had gone way too far, but what else could they do, they needed her testimony to have any chance of getting those bastards. Minutes passed as everyone waited for something to happen.

"That's it; I'm calling the local police." The doctor threatened, turn to leave.

"Good. You can mention to them, how this guard told us they have been using the patients for oral sex." Ross pointed out, seeing the doctor's face go white, as his guards looked to their injured companion.

"Ross, let it go, there's no need for any more trouble, we're going," Dave replied standing up dejectedly. He knew that even with Ross' threat about charging the guards, they'd probably lose their badges for this mess. The worst of it was, it had been for nothing. Defeated he stood up and turned to when the girls arm shot out, grabbing his sleeve.

"Don't go!" came a guttural croak. Eva as if waking from an evil filled nightmare, started to shake uncontrollably. Dave taken aback by her voice grabbed a blanket from a rack beside the bed. Wrapping her in it, he sat down next to her holding her to him. From the doorway, the Doctor with a hand gesture, signalled everyone to be quiet, as he looked on as if witnessing a vision.

"I'm so frightened all the time; I'm scared to close my eyes." She whispered, tears flowing down her face as she continued to shake. "I can't remember what happened clearly, it's all jumbled up in my head." She cried out desperately wanting someone to believe her.

"You're safe now Eva. What's the last thing you remember?" Dave said softly, tears starting to form in his eyes. At first, he thought he'd lost her, as she'd returned to her safe place hiding inside herself, going blank. Moments later after another fit of shaking, she started to talk.

"I went to the Dean's house to play for him and Doctor Clark. I was a gifted pianist." She stuttered out wiping her eyes, continuing. "The Dean gave me something to drink, orange juice I think, and then everything went black. They raped me didn't they?" Eva screamed, bursting into tears, sobbing as if her chest would cave in. All present looked on silently, as the Doctor waved his men away.

"Yes Eva, we believe they did after drugging you," Dave confessed.

"I went there to play for them, why would they hurt me?" She continued to cry. Dave knew she wanted to know the reason for her brutal treatment, he knew there was no answer. Seeing the detective was unable to reply she moved on.

"I can't remember anything solid there are only fragments of two men doing terrible things to me." She cried, her voice sounding as if she was reliving the whole ordeal.

"I'm so sorry for what they did to you Eva, at least now we can stop them," Dave replied holding her hand, as she came into his arms hugging him, making him shake with her gut-wrenching sobs.

"They've done it to others haven't they?" Eva asked coming suddenly alert, looking Dave straight in the eye.

"Yes many more, unfortunately, how did you know?" Dave asked softly.

"When they had me, I remember them taking a break, watching a movie of them raping someone else. When they'd finished watching it, they returned to me." She confessed sobbing again. The absolute horror of what she'd been through covered the men standing there with revulsion. All of them for some time weren't able to look at Eva. Standing wiping his face, Dave didn't know what to say.

"Stop them, Dave, before they hurt someone else," Eva whispered, collapsing back onto the bed exhausted.

"That, I can assure you," Dave promised, looking down at Eva feeling somehow guilty for her ordeal.

"Can someone ring my mum, I want to see her!" Eva moaned, hiding her face in a pillow. Ushering the two detectives outside, the doctor indicated that Eva needed to rest.

"This is a miracle. I never thought I would hear her talk again." The Doctor confessed happily. "God I can't believe you broke through to her after all this time. I'd say she'll make a full recovery with time." He continued smiling.

"Keep her safe doctor? She's now a material witness in a murder case." Ross told him.

"She also deserves to be treated better after what she's been through." Dave pointed out, looking towards the door where the injured guard sat with the other guards. Seeing what he was looking at, the Doctor turned to him.

"He won't cause any trouble again, I'll have him moved. Your methods might be a bit over the top detective, but this time they worked." He smiled. "You'd better get going; you've got those monsters to catch." Shaking the doctor's hand was in a way an apology for his treatment, as they hurriedly left.

Jumping into the car they quickly rang Lismore station, getting their boss to get a search warrant rolling. If he could get that done, they'd meet the Sydney detectives at Clark's house in three hour's time. Hanging up, Ross gunned the engine heading south.

"Put the siren on Ross. I said three hours not thirty." Dave ordered his voice devoid of emotion. Ross picked up on his anger hit the switch, racing through the traffic.

THE SOLUTION

The night before Detective Johnson and Detective Luke drove north to interview Eva, Clark and Davison arrived home from work. They were no fools and had seen the police tailing them both, on the way home.

"They're on to us!" Davison put forward, as they both sat down enjoying a sherry.

"I can't understand why they didn't find the gun at Michael's farm?" Clark asked sounding confused.

"Maybe they didn't even go there as the call was anonymous? We'll have to do something quickly to get the cops out there to search their place." Davison suggested knowing the cops would continue to look at them unless they got a break.

"It'll have to be at night my friend, or otherwise the cops watching here will see us." Clark pointed out.

"I'd even suggest going tonight. The more time goes by, the more likely the cops will zero in on us." Davison replied.

"It won't be easy, we can't possibly get past them in a car, and we can't walk to Michael's farm," Clark added.

"No problems, we'll go over through the back paddock and walk to the University. I can borrow one of the staff cars from there before we drive out to their farm." Davison suggested smiling.

"Good thinking. Once there, something should present itself." Clark smiled, as they walked upstairs to make ready. "Another problem, what if they want to search here?" Clark asked as they walked to their rooms.

"When we get back, I think we should have a fire, maybe something left on the stove?" Davison suggested chuckling insanely.

"Not all the films I hope?" Clark asked surprised.

"No, those we'll bury out on the property somewhere. The main thing is to destroy anything here we might have missed." Davison informed him as they went into their rooms and changed.

The four friends ate their meal in silence all pondering what tomorrow would bring. Detective Luke had rung earlier explaining how the samples had been tampered with. He also told them the finding of another girl, who'd given a recital for Clark and Davison, had been found. At first, the friends had been overcome with joy hoping finally something would be done about Bella's torturers. Michael wasn't too sure.

He pointed out that all the evidence was still circumstantial; unless the girl could actually testify that she witnessed something. Judging by what they did to Bella, he doubted it.

Bella listening sat silently as a growing sense of frustration gripped her. Leaving the table, she decided to clean up the kitchen rather than sit a moment longer. Washing up, she heard her three friends arguing over their next course of action. Getting angry she reached into the sink water, cutting her hand on a carving knife.

Letting out a cry of pain, her friends instantly appeared at the door wondering what was wrong. Examining her wound, Jed suggested he take her to the hospital to see if she needed stitches. Michael agreeing gave Jed the keys to his car, telling him to be careful. Waving goodbye Michael hugging Kirra walked back inside to clean up when a banging noise came from the farm shed where they kept their tools.

"Bugger! Must have left the door unlocked, I'll go close it and hurry back." Michael smiled, giving Kirra a passionate kiss while running his hands up her thigh.

"Well looks like someone wants something?" She giggled, giving him a seductive pose, as he hurriedly left laughing. Quickly cleaning up the kitchen she hurried to her room changing out of her clothing. Standing naked she looked at her reflection, smiling as her excitement grew. Putting on a flimsy silk dressing gown, she walked out onto the front veranda to await his return.

As Michael neared the barn, he silently cursed Jed for being so casual. Jed had been down the shed in the afternoon working on their tractor. He'd run over some barbwire, tangling it in the slasher's blades. Obviously in his hurry, he'd forgotten the door. Walking up to the barn he saw the lock lying on the ground.

"That's funny Jed was casual, but he wouldn't leave the lock on the ground," Michael said to himself, as bending over to pick up the lock, he saw the blur of a shovel coming towards him. Reacting, he tried to move back out of the way, but it connected, knocking him to the ground. Still conscious he tried to stand only to be hit again this time knocking him out.

Clark and Davison had arrived just after dark at Michael's farm. Driving past the entrance, they'd parked along the rear boundary, in a small group of gum trees. Looking around, seeing the area was deserted they walked across the farm through the orchard, using the fruit trees to hide their movement. Watching from the cover of darkness they saw the four young adults enjoying dinner.

Moving closer, they were just about to approach the house when Jed and Bella came out onto the veranda climbing into a ute and driving off. Retreating to the cover of the trees they waited as Jed drove past them down to the road heading towards town. Now hiding in the shadows the two men planned their next move.

"We've got to separate them. On their own, they'll be easy meat." Clark whispered excitedly.

"Let's go back to the shed we passed, I've got an idea." Davison chuckled, moving back the way they came. Coming to the shed Davison picked up a piece of metal putting it through the chain and breaking the lock. Letting the door swing in the breeze, he hit the shed wall several times.

"Hide inside, whoever comes hit them over the head," Davison ordered smiling, as Clark grabbed a shovel from inside and waited in the door's shadow. Several minutes passed as a shadow appeared, walking towards the barn. Clark recognised Michael talking to himself, as he moved to the shed door. Bending down to pick up the lock, Clark saw his chance and swung the shovel hitting him. He went down but continued struggling, so he hit him again in the forehead. This time he stayed down.

"That was easy!" Clark chuckled about to swing again and kill Michael.

"Don't kill him here." Davison stopped him "We don't want any blood down here. He dies up there with the whore." He continued smiling.

"Good thinking. We can make it look like Michael went crazy, raping and butchering Bella's girlfriend." Clark replied his eyes shining with the thought of another plaything.

"Grab his legs; we'll carry him to the house," Davison said seriously, as they hauled him to his feet. After carrying Michael to the house, they moved him round to the back door dropping him outside. Carefully circling around they spotted Kirra on the front veranda standing waiting for Michael. In her brief dressing gown with the light behind her, she appeared naked to the two men who stood mesmerised.

"What a lovely young woman. She'll make a great plaything." Clark whispered, as Davison beside him wet his lips.

"Let's get her my friend; this is going to be fun." Davison giggled out loud.

Kirra on the veranda became concerned that Michael had not returned from the barn. She was just about to go looking for him when the sound of someone giggling softly came to her from the shadows.

"Who's there? Is that you Michael?" Kirra yelled, her voice cracking with fear as no answer came. The darkness seemed to move closer to the veranda, as fear made her slowly back up moving inside the doorway. Scared now, wondering what was out there, Kirra looked at the side of the veranda to see Doctor Clark's face staring at her.

Screaming with mind-numbing fear, Kirra rushed inside slamming the door and locking it. Looking around, crying in fear she watched the handle on the front door turn.

"The phone!" she said out loud, as Clark tried to force open the door behind her. Racing into the kitchen, she grabbed her phone, as the door behind her caved in. Knowing she wouldn't have time to dial, she raced for the back door deciding to try and get away. As she cleared the doorway, a hand shot out grabbing her hair, bringing her to a painful abrupt halt.

"Nearly made it didn't you!" Davison snarled in her ear, ripping her dressing gown from her body and squeezing her breast painfully. Too scared even to reply, Kirra, shaking with fear re-lived her ordeal inflicted by her uncle. Seeing her terror, Davison laughed insanely, feasting on it. Dragging her back into the house, he waited for Clark.

"Where's Michael?" She whimpered, as Davison pushed her up against the kitchen sink letting her feel how excited he was.

"He's okay at the moment. If he stays that way, is up to you!" He chuckled, watching her cower as his hands explored her body.

"Good you got her!" Clark exclaimed coming in the back door staring ravenously at Kirra's body. "Got the front door opened, but it fell onto the dining table, stopping me from getting in," Clark explained, moving swiftly towards Kirra. Taking Davison's place, he bent her over slapping her backside viciously, before biting it painfully. Groaning in agony, Kirra unable to break free, screamed, praying someone would help her. In reply Clark banged her head on the bench, tossing her onto the floor, as both men stripped off their clothes.

"Crawl over here bitch, or I'll slit your boyfriend's throat," Clark shouted, saliva spraying from his mouth, as Davison laughed hysterically.

"Come on plaything, we're both waiting," Davison added gleefully dropping his pants to the ground. Lying on the floor shaking, Kirra cringed into a corner. The hopelessness of her situation made her sob uncontrollably as the two men stripped completely before advancing towards her.

"Please don't hurt us!" Kirra begged them, as Clark stared down at her smiling. Grabbing a handful of Kirra's hair, he dragged her head between his legs.

"Well that's up to you, isn't it. Let's see how good you can perform." He laughed. Kirra looking up trembled with fear and revulsion, as she stared at his rigid member, inches from her face. Trying to buy Michael and herself more time she readied herself to comply. Opening her mouth she breathed in the feral smell of Clark's unwashed genitals, causing her to vomit. Clark looking down expectantly, gasped in surprise as Kirra emptied her stomach over his legs.

"You filthy little slut!" Clark screamed, slapping her hard across the face, as he jumped back. Looking down at the mess she'd made, he angrily ripped down the window curtains, wiping himself. Davison beside him thrust his leg forward, kicking her in the stomach, making her fall back onto the garbage bin. Crying hysterically she held her stomach trying to stop the pain.

"Are you okay?" Davison asked his friend, helping wipe the mess off his legs.

"I'm okay, though I think our plaything better crawl back over here and apologise, or her boyfriend out there is going to die horribly," Clark promised pointing at his penis, making Davison giggle. Kirra terrified too scared to reply, placed her hands in front of her preparing to start crawling towards them. Her right hand came to rest on the rubbish from the bin.

Feeling something solid, Kirra, looked down seeing Michael's shotgun lying amongst the garbage. In a fit of desperation, she pulled it up from the floor pointing it at the two men, before pulling both triggers at the same time.

Davison at first thought she was complying with Clark's instructions when he saw the gun appear in her hands from nowhere.

"No!" he screamed, as Clark beside him stared at his friend surprised. He had been so engrossed with her obeying him that his whole concentration had been on Kirra's body, not her hands. The blast came as an exploding roar of noise and motion as hundreds of small pellets fanned out towards the back door. The blast hit both men propelling them out through the doorway gutting them both. Kirra too was thrown backwards, as the two barrels exploded. They propelled her into the dining room, the butt of the weapon hitting her across the shoulder, before cannoning into her jaw, knocking her unconscious.

Michael who through all this, had lain outside knocked out, slowly came to, as a sea of noise came to him getting increasingly louder. Climbing up from the ground standing unsteadily, he made his way towards the garbled sounds. As his hearing returned, and he moved closer, Michael heard someone crying for help. In the background, the guttural sounds of someone moaning in agony could also be distinguished. Stopping abruptly forgetting the sounds, Michael realised that he'd been attacked.

Becoming more cautious he again moved forward the realisation that Kirra was alone, driving him onwards. Coming to the front door, he saw the damage, though unlike Clark he managed to climb over the wreckage. The first thing he saw was Kirra lying naked at the entrance to the kitchen.

"Kirra!" Michael cried in panic. Running to her, he checked her breathing, checking for wounds. Watching her chest rise and fall, he breathed a sigh of relief, crying with pent-up fear. Moving her to the lounge he made her comfortable before entering the kitchen. The first thing he saw was the shotgun, looking beyond, he saw Clark and Davison dying on the back steps.

"Help me!" Davison begged from the rear door, as Michael emptied his stomach onto the kitchen floor. Frozen by the absolute horror that had filled his home, Michael stared with contempt at Davison.

"Help me." He pleaded, moaning in agony.

"Burn in hell you bastard!" Michael screamed back, as he turned away from the dying monsters, going back to Kirra. Sitting down he cradled her, as Davison's cries for help grew softer, and Clark's moaning ceased.

Jed drove up the driveway, as Bella beside him sang along with a tune on the radio. Bella's hand hadn't needed stitching, so the two had slowly driven back home, enjoying each other's company.

"So much for locking up! Michael's left the front door wide open." Bella giggled. Jed beside her smiled, as he too looked towards the door. His smile fled, as he saw the door lying on an angle across the dining table.

"Stay in the car and lock the doors," Jed ordered, as jumping out of the Ute he grabbed a tyre wrench from the rear tray. Advancing slowly, he looked inside seeing

Michael and Kirra sitting traumatised on the lounge. Signalling to Bella to stay put, he walked inside, passing his two friends who didn't even acknowledge him. Looking in the kitchen, he saw what was left of Clark and Davison near the rear door.

"Holy shit!" he said out loud before retracing his steps. Approaching the car, Jed vomited onto the road, as Bella inside rolled into a ball holding her legs against her chest, knowing something terrible had occurred. Jed recovering came around to her window, signalling her to open it. Explaining what he had found, Bella burst into tears, before to Jed's surprise she rushed inside. Once beside her friend she lifted Kirra walking her outside onto the veranda.

"Bring Michael!" she ordered, as Jed obeyed carrying Michael out as well. At first, Kirra just sat there frozen, as Bella tried to rally her. In the end, Bella slapped her face, forcing her from her emotional hiding place. Kirra immediately screamed as if the devil himself was attacking her. Holding and comforting her, Bella held on until Kirra's screams subsided becoming sobs of anguish. Michael in time returned to the present, telling Jed what had occurred crying in absolute misery at what he'd let happen to Kirra.

"It wasn't your fault mate, it was all theirs." Jed pointed out, thinking how close these monsters had again come to destroying their family.

"What are we going to do?" Michael asked scared to look inside the house.

"We've got to get rid of them. The cops can't find them here." Jed replied, knowing the cops wouldn't take kindly to two men being killed by an illegal gun. "Look I'll get some blankets and cover them. You can help me drag them out back." Jed volunteered walking inside.

It was a hideous mess Jed realised, as he threw a blanket over each man. Moving closer, his stomach dry reaching, Jed struggled to try to wrap the badly slashed bodies. Michael suddenly appeared beside him, helping him drag the bodies outside. Michael, then grabbed an outside hose, spraying water over the entire kitchen.

This cleared away the rest of the mess and blood, making the place at least presentable if not heavily damaged.

"What now?" Michael asked, his head bleeding from his attack earlier.

"First we'll fix that wound of yours, and then we'll make sure Kirra is alright," Jed suggested, moving Michael into the bathroom. Kirra and Bella were already there, Kirra lying in a warm bath naked, bruises on her face and body clearly visible.

"Is she okay?" Jed asked Bella softly.

"I'm fine Jed. Its … it's just I was so terrified, I thought after they finished with me, Michael and I would both be murdered in a brutal agonising way." She stammered out, shaking with fear.

"I'm sorry Kirra that I wasn't here to protect you." Michael sobbed, as Kirra climbed out of the bath hugging him to her.

"You have nothing to be sorry about. They knocked you out Michael you couldn't do anything. They wanted me to do their bidding before they killed us both. Luckily the shotgun was in the bin, or they would've succeeded." Kirra admitted hopping back into the warmth of the bath. Bella seeing Kirra was recovering grabbed the first aid kit, bandaging Michael's wound. Finished Michael and Jed went out to the veranda to think about what to do next.

"We've got to get rid of those bodies and quick!" Jed blurted out, worried that with all the noise tonight, at any moment the police might turn up.

"I thought of something while we were working. They must have a car somewhere. If we can find it, we could

drive them both somewhere else and dump them."
Michael suggested.

"Good idea. You clean yourself up, I'll go look along
the boundaries, see if I can find it." Jed answered
grabbing a torch and leaving. It took Jed an hour to locate
the car, by this time it was close to eleven at night and
pitch dark.

So confident were Clark and Davison of their plan
succeeding, they'd left the keys in the ignition for a quick
departure. Starting the car making sure no one was
around, Jed drove up to the house, driving around the
back. Getting out he found Michael waiting. Without
delay, he opened the rear door of their car, shoving the
two bodies inside.

"Right, it might be best if I drive them, while you follow
in your car." Jed volunteered, as Michael grateful,
thanked him. It was a long drive for Jed as his two
companions moved from side to side in the rear seat
every time he turned a corner. Getting freaked out by the
whole thing, Jed put his foot down racing through the
night, Michael always right behind him.

Coming to a bad corner marked by a sign indicating a
sharp right-hand bend, Jed drove across the road onto
the verge of a steep cliff. Jumping out, he looked down at
the dark water flowing far below him, preparing himself
for the next step. Michael parking around the corner
hurried back coming up beside Jed.

"The river's pretty deep here, let's roll her over the
edge and get out of here before someone comes," Jed
suggested, sounding scared as they both put their
shoulders into pushing the car. At first the car fought
them refusing to budge; in the end, Jed having had
enough wedged a stick behind the accelerator before
dropping it into gear. With a mighty roar, the car surged
forward, as Jed jumping out, watched the car fall into
nothingness, vanishing into the water below.

"Fuck that wasn't easy!" Jed spat out as in the distance the sound of a car approaching could be heard.

"Run to the car let's get out of here," Michael screamed as the two friends, hurtled down the road to Michael's Ute. Diving into it and starting it, Michael swung the car around, heading back the way they'd come, as lights appeared in their rear window.

"Don't let them get close enough to see our number plate!" Jed yelled, as Michael way ahead of him, flattened the accelerator, racing away into the night.

Arriving home sure they hadn't been seen they both collapsed onto the front veranda sitting down silently letting the adrenaline leave their systems.

"That was close!" Jed smiled, for the first time that night, as they both closed their eyes, sleeping where they sat. The next morning the two women emerged from Bella's room. Coming out onto the veranda they found their men asleep. Kirra wanting to put her ordeal behind her pulled Michael to his feet leading him to her bed, as Bella followed suit with Jed. Stripping him, Kirra lay beside Michael, calming her beating heart, trying to forget the terror. They made love several times that day, no one wanting to leave the safety of their beds. In the end, at about 2 in the afternoon, they all emerged from their places of safety, to put the kitchen and the rest of their home back in order.

WANTED

Dave and Ross checked their weapons, taking the safeties off. With several Swat Team members, they advanced on Davison's house. Kicking in the front and back doors at the same time, police swarmed into the house, tearing it apart.

"They're not here!" Dave bellowed in rage, wondering where the detectives from Sydney assigned to watch the house, were. Later they'd find out they went to dinner in town, leaving the house unguarded.

"I'll check the garage out back while you find that room," Ross suggested taking two men with him. It wasn't long before Dave found the hidden entrance with the help of a sledgehammer. Slowly walking down the stairs gun held out in front, Dave secretly hoped they were hiding here so he could finish them. Instead, he found a place riddled with untold horrors carried out by unfeeling animals. Going to a side table, Dave looked at the large collection of DVDs held in a rack beside the oversized bed. Each one had a name and dates, some going back several years.

Looking at nothing, in particular, Dave spotted a date that made him wince; it was the day Ross' girl Jenny had disappeared. Putting it in the DVD player, Dave and the Swat members present watched Clark and Davison rape Ross' poor defenceless daughter. Fast-forwarding it, trying to get to the end, they watched Clark and Davison strangle her. Holding back tears, Dave grabbed the disk destroying it. No one said anything, the Swat members affected as badly as Dave.

"Someone's got to tell him." the Sergeant in charge of Swat team whispered, as all eyes turned to Dave.

"I'll do it. Make sure no one else sees these tapes." Dave ordered, wiping his face, before going upstairs looking for Ross. Emerging into the backyard, Dave

watched as the two men sent with Ross hurried across to
him.

"There's something wrong with Detective Luke Sir?
He's crying in the garage." One of the men told him sadly,
not knowing what was wrong.

"I'll handle it, you men report to your Sergeant," Dave
ordered walking towards the garage. He found Ross
sitting quietly inside, beside a brown coloured van. In his
hands was a ripped dress covered with dried blood.

"She bought this dress for the New Year's Eve party.
Jenny thought we didn't know she was wearing this one
that night, putting on another one to please us. She was
going to that party to really let her hair down, she was so
excited. I should have said something to slow her down,
but she was so stubborn, like me." Ross sobbed, looking
ten years older.

"Let's get you out of here mate. This is no place for
you at the moment." Dave suggested as tears ran down
his partner's face. Ross getting to his feet, let Dave lead
him to their car. Telling the swat members to secure the
buildings he drove Ross home. Grabbing his radio as he
drove, he called in what they'd found issuing orders to put
roadblocks on all roads within a hundred kilometres of
Lismore. He then asked his boss to do a television
appearance, explaining two homicidal murders were on
the loose.

Dropping Ross home, Dave rushed into the station to
find the media frenzy had started. Photos of the two men
were on display, along with a description of a car stolen
from the University. The Inspector seeing Dave waved
him through the crowd, leading him to his room.

"How bad is it?" the Inspector asked.

"They've been at it for years Sir. Ross's daughter was
one of their first victims." Dave croaked out, wiping his
eyes. The Inspector at first seemed too shocked to reply,
knowing how they'd all been deceived by these monsters.

"I don't care what it takes or where they go, I want these men dead. Is that understood Detective?" The Inspector ordered his anger evident.

"You can count on that Sir, but these guys are smart. They may have already skipped the country." Dave admitted sadly.

"Do your best my friend and give my best to Ross, anything he needs ring me." The Inspector said softly.

"Thanks, Sir I'll get moving," Dave replied hurrying out to coordinate the search.

For the next six months, every Police Force in Australia turned the country upside down, looking for the two murderers. Both the men and the car seemed to have been swallowed by the earth itself as every lead was tracked down. Ross had broken down altogether, needing several months off having relived the horror of his daughter's kidnapping. Finding out tapes had been made of the torture of their victims and they were being kept as evidence, caused an uproar.

The relations of the victims wanted them destroyed, but the chief magistrate wanted them as evidence. Several days passed before a mysterious fire destroyed them all. Ross returned soon afterwards thanking Dave for the fire.

"I didn't do it. It occurred just after I left the evidence locker." Dave answered, knowing the brass weren't happy with the fire.

"So where are we in the investigation?" Ross asked neutrally.

"I don't know mate, there have been no sightings at all, they're either bunkered down somewhere remote or dead," Dave answered truthfully.

"I'd prefer the second, but I'd love to find them," Ross replied his eyes distant, looking at something in the past.

"Don't worry I'll never stop looking," Dave replied his voice full of emotion, as Ross moved past Dave into their office.

"Then let's recheck everything, just in case." Ross smiled opening Clark's file.

The Farm

Life for Michael and the others improved with time, as the people who had ostracised them, admitted they'd been wrong. Using his last reserve of funds, Michael rebuilt the kitchen, burning the old one. Kirra was at first scared to stay on her own, although recovered, she never ventured far from the others. Life improved for them, as they again sold their crops locally, even managing to put some away for the future.

Every now and then they saw Detective Johnson and Detective Luke, who kept them up to date with the search for Davison and Clark. Detective Luke, or Ross, as they now called him, seem attentive of Bella, always asking how she was. Jed hearing how Ross' daughter, had been murdered by Clark and Davison saw the connection. To Ross, Bella had become his de-facto daughter he watched over her now keeping his distance, just making sure she was safe.

Another year passed, and the murders were all but forgotten, when a bunch of school kids having too much to drink, rolled their car on a bad corner south of the town. Luckily they all got out, though the car was a write-off. To stop the pollution of the river, a local crane was brought in, to lift the car clear of the river. Lowering a large hook into the water, the crane immediately snagged a vehicle. Lifting it clear, to everyone's amazement, they realized they'd snagged a different vehicle.

"You may as well lift it clear, I'm sure the council will pay to have it removed as well." the Young Constable assigned to traffic control at the corner, informed the crane driver. As the vehicle was lifted onto the roadside, the constable curious rubbed the license plates, hoping to check on its identity. Cleaning it with a piece of rag the constable stared at the plate wondering why the plate seemed familiar when recognition hit him.

"Don't touch anything, everybody back." The Constable roared, startling the gathered crowd. Running to his car, he called Lismore station informing them that Clark and Davison's missing car had been found. In less than ten minutes, the small crowd gathered were scattered by the arrival of police cars from all over the area. Cordoning off the entire area, the road was closed as Dave and Ross screamed to a halt, practically jumping from their car.

"Has anyone touched it?" Dave yelled.

"No when I saw the plates I kept everyone away." the Young Constable confessed, knowing these two detective's reputation for anger.

"Good work Officer." Dave smiled moving slowly forward, Ross beside him. The windows were coated with mud, and the inside seemed to have filled up with sediment.

"It's hard to see inside Ross. Has anyone here got a paint scraper?" Dave shouted out to the crowd as one bystander, fetched one from his work vehicle. Ross thanking the man returned to the vehicle. Swiftly clearing a patch in the front window, they tried to peer in. Seeing nothing, Dave then scraped the rear window on the passenger's side. As he scraped away the muck, he suddenly saw before him the skeletal remains of a man's head.

"Holy Shit!" he yelled, jumping back in shock, as Ross moved closer.

"Looks like there's two of them when you look closely,"
Ross informed him, as Dave recovered, had a closer
look.

"You're right, it is two heads. Do you think they killed
themselves?" Dave asked softly, finding it hard to believe.

"I doubt it, they didn't seem the type. There is only one
way to find out. Let's get a forensic team in here." Ross
suggested smiling, remembering Dave's last clash with
them.

It took two days for the team to arrive, setting up in a
vacant warehouse in town. The vehicle was then carefully
moved there, while divers brought in from Sydney,
painstakingly checked the riverbed for any evidence as to
what had happened. After a week of examining the
vehicle, the Forensic team had pieced together a rough
idea as to what had taken place. After reading the report,
Dave and Ross sat speechless wondering what had
occurred.

"So while naked, they were shot at point-blank range
by someone lying on the ground, which they were facing.
They were then wrapped in blankets and driven to the
river where the vehicle was deliberately driven over the
cliff." Dave said out loud, digesting the report.

"Yeah, and the weapon recovered, had both its barrels
fired at the same time. I'm glad it wasn't me being shot,
or the shooter for that matter. He must've received quite
a wack from that gun." Ross replied smiling.

"I don't get it. Both men were predators. It's hard to
believe someone got the drop on them." Dave pointed
out, confused.

"The person was either on the ground or close to it by
the angle of the pellet wounds, maybe they were lying in
wait for them." Ross put forward.

"No that would be premeditated, meaning the killer had
planned it. No one would plan something like this and

then be stupid enough to fire both barrels at once. Whoever did this hadn't fired a gun before; I'd say the Doc, and the Dean may have been attacking someone who grabbed a gun to defend themselves at the last minute." Dave suggested thinking about it.

"That fits Dave. It explains why the person fired from ground level, instead of being upright, and why they both were naked." Ross smiled, thinking they were getting somewhere. Going over the pictures of the shotgun, Dave noticed something odd about it.

"Hey look at the firing mechanism. It's made of brass, as is the trigger and they've been engraved with small animals. There can't be many shotguns made like that about. I'd say it could have been a special order." Dave exclaimed, knowing weapons like this one could be tracked.

"I'll go to records, see if it's got a history," Ross replied knowing they were getting closer to solving the mystery.

Three days of searching and a tired Ross found what he was looking for. A shotgun matching the description of the one they'd recovered was stolen from a farm south of Lismore, over thirty years ago. The only other reference to that particular type of gun was that it or something similar was used in several holdups. Checking arrests at the time, Ross found that Michael's father had been convicted for some of these robberies and had been using such a weapon, though it was never recovered. Going to Dave's office, Ross told him what he'd found.

"Could be just a coincidence," Ross added, trying to water down what he was thinking.

"Look, Ross, I know those four have been through hell, but I've got to bring Michael in to answer some questions," Dave replied. He too was reluctant to cause them more grief.

"Let me do it. One of us going out there should be enough." Ross volunteered. Dave seeing he wanted to, gave him the nod.

Driving up the driveway to Michael's farm, Ross felt the guilt of the belting they'd given both Jed and Michael at the station resurface. Pulling up, Ross hesitated wishing he hadn't come. Getting over it, knowing it had to be done, he jumped out of the car walking to the veranda. Knocking on the door, Ross waited. Getting no answer he went around the back, walking up the three steps, he knocked on the rear door to the kitchen.

Looking inside, he noticed Michael had replaced his kitchen, installing one of those kitchens that you build yourself. It wasn't a bad job he thought, moving back down the stairs, he prepared to leave. Looking down at the ground, Ross stopped, as something caught his eye in the grass at the bottom of the steps.

Reaching down he picked up a small round piece of lead. Feeling around he found several more, as his guts tightened. Retracing his steps he went round to the front opening the door. He was just about to enter when Michael's Utility came up the drive towards him.

"Hey, Ross" Bella greeted him, as the others more reluctantly said their hellos.

"How are you all going?" Ross replied, smiling. Getting a brief rundown on what had been happening, the group's conversation trailed off as they waited to find out why he was here.

"I've just got a couple of questions for Michael. Won't take long," He assured them. Guarded looks passed between the four, as Kirra, Bella and Jed drifted inside. Michael sat down on the veranda offering Ross a seat which he accepted.

"Look I don't know if you'd heard, but Clark and Davison's bodies have been found in a car dumped in the river," Ross informed him.

"Yeah, we heard it on the news," Michael replied, adding nothing else.

"Well what people don't know, is it wasn't a suicide, both men were murdered. Someone blew them away with a shotgun." Ross told him, seeing Michael's eyes take on a hunted look.

"Hey, I don't know anything about it man." Michael blurted out, "I don't even own a gun." He added.

"I'm not pointing the finger at anyone Michael: as far as I'm concerned, they got what they deserved. The problem is that the gun was the same type used by your father in some bank robberies." Ross revealed. Michael for some time sat there silently as Ross waited for an answer.

"Must be just a coincidence." Michael finally answered.

"Okay then, that's all I needed to know. Someone, of course, will have to talk to your father, but we won't bother you again." Ross smiled. Both getting up, Michael walked Ross to his car saying goodbye. Driving down the road, Ross looked back to see Michael still standing where he'd left him, and a premonition of trouble hitting him.

Back at the station, Dave watched Ross bypass his office, going into his own. Giving his partner ten minutes to sort himself out, Dave getting up went to Ross' office, to find him sitting at his desk staring out the window.

"How'd it go?" Dave asked startling Ross.

"Okay. He didn't know anything." Ross replied sounding vague.

"What gives Ross? You're not telling me everything!" Dave asked. Ross at first said nothing. Seeing Dave knew he was hiding something, he showed him the small lead pellets. Dave looked at them, then at Ross.

"Where'd you find them?" He asked.

"It doesn't prove anything really. They could be from any shotgun. It's just Michael put in a whole new kitchen, and these pellets were outside on the ground near the steps. He also lied and said he didn't have a gun" Ross admitted.

"Do you think those two sickos could've gone to Michael's farm and been shot by either Jed or Michael?" Dave whispered.

"No I don't think the boys shot them, they'd know not to pull both triggers. We also know the shot came from the ground." Ross reminded him. Dave thought over what Ross had said coming to a conclusion.

"What if Clark and Davison went after one of the girls. What if while they had her on the floor, she somehow grabbed the gun and finished them." Dave put forward. Ross didn't reply thinking of his daughter. Dave seeing his look left him returning to his own office. 'Fuck what a mess.' Dave thought wondering how to proceed as Ross appeared at his door.

"It ends now Dave! I won't give those poor bastards any more grief." Ross thundered, surprising Dave.

"I wasn't going to do anything mate. I don't give a rat's arse about who killed them. It's just if we found the connection, someone else will. So what do we do?" Dave asked.

"We go interview Michael's dad then dead end it. Put it down as a double suicide that should stop others looking." Ross suggested.

"Sounds good, we'll do that. Then it's over." Dave replied, concerned for Ross.

GRAFTON PRISON

Michael's dad, Eric, was being held at Grafton prison in Grafton two hour's drive south of Lismore. He had been held in Sydney at a high-security prison for the last eight years. Because he only had a couple more years to serve, he'd been moved to the low-security jail, pending his release.

The trip south to the jail was mostly in silence as the two detectives thought about the coming interview. Both had looked at Eric's record. He was a real low life if he'd been out they'd have pinned these murders on him in a minute. Unfortunately being in jail gave you a pretty tight alibi. Waiting in the interview room behind a wall of glass Dave and Ross watched Eric prance in as if he owned the place.

"What the fuck do you two want?" Eric snarled, slouching down into the chair opposite them.

"Good to see you too, Eric. We've got a couple of questions for you." Ross informed him.

"Go ahead flatfoot. I've got all the time in the world." Eric smirked.

"What happened to the shotgun you used in all those robberies?" Dave asked.

"Haven't the faintest what you're talking about." Eric smiled.

Shoving a picture of the shotgun through the bars, Dave watched his reaction. His smiling face disappeared as his eyes went wide.

"This gun was used in a double murder recently. Look familiar?" Dave asked.

"Never seen the gun before, so if that's all you've got, you can both fuck off, I'm going!" Eric replied, jumping to his feet, his hostility plain to see.

"I thought you had plenty of time?" Dave smiled, as Eric walked away, giving them the finger.

"He certainly recognised the gun." Ross smiled.

"Yeah, he certainly did. I wondered why he went ballistic like that." Dave mused, getting up. The interview was obviously finished.

Leaving the detectives, Eric walked back to his cell his black mood radiating malaise as other prisons moved out of his path. He knew if someone had that gun, they had his money, and he wanted blood. Sitting in his cell, he thought back to the night he hid the gun and his money. There was no way anyone could have seen him hide it, and his family still lived there, so who'd discovered it?

As if lightning had struck him, he remembered throwing the shovel against the shed where that little bastard had slept. 'He must have seen me' Eric thought, remembering how his son had told him several years ago that Michael had come into some money buying a farm.

"That little fuck. I'll see him dead for this. That's after I get my money back!" Eric exploded. The prison block around him grew quiet as the other inmates sensed that Eric was about to lose it. The clever ones found somewhere else to be. A blind man could see trouble was coming. Pulling a brick loose from behind his bed he pulled out an illegal phone his sons had smuggled in. Ringing them, he told them he was breaking out, telling them of the money Michael had taken.

Arranging for them to meet him at the local hospital, he put one of his emergency plans into action. In his illegal stash, he also had a small hunting knife. Putting it in his pocket, he put the phone and the rest of his possessions back in the hiding place. Standing up, he stood near his doorway waiting for his mark. The flow of prisoners passed his cell had dwindled to only the toughest since his outburst, which suited him just fine. He knew he needed a big bastard to justify his plan. Looking down the corridor, he saw a prisoner named Brody coming towards him.

Brody enjoyed prison. He enjoyed the power he had here and his appetite for young men. He had once been a heavyweight boxer, big and powerful, but the scars on his face showed that despite his size he hadn't been too successful. Coming up to Eric, Brody saw him staring at him issuing a challenge with his eyes.

"What the fuck, are you looking at dickhead?" Brody asked crossing his arms, showing Eric his huge biceps.

"A dead man!" Eric smiled. Swiftly pulling his knife from his pocket, he slashed at Brody's neck. Taken completely by surprise Brody reacted a second too slow as the knife cut deeply into his throat. Blood sprayed over the corridor as Brody, in panic, tried to halt the flow holding his throat, screaming out. Eric moving away reversed his knife driving it repeatedly into his arms and stomach, screaming as well. Brody, losing his fight for life, collapsed onto the floor as Eric feeling himself becoming dizzy reached down to Brody placing the knife in Brody's hand.

By this time, the screams and yells from the prison block had sent the prison into lockdown. Ten guards in riot gear, rushed down the corridor to investigate. Summoning medical personnel, the guards did what they could for Eric. It was too late for Brody.

"What happened?" A guard asked Eric.

"He came at me with a knife, I managed to push him away and cut him. I didn't mean to kill him, I was defending myself." Eric replied, convincingly. Most of the guards didn't believe the bullshit he was feeding them, but he was badly hurt. Doubts aside, they did their job patching him up. Getting him stable enough to travel, they arranged transport for him. Under guard, Eric was escorted to the local hospital.

Dave and Ross driving back to Lismore tried to puzzle out Eric's reaction to their questioning. They could understand his denying any involvement in the shooting, but his anger when seeing the weapon had surprised them.

"He acted like someone had stolen it from him." Dave put forward.

"Yeah I know people get attached to their guns, but that's ridiculous." Ross smiled.

"Do you think Michael took it?" Dave asked softly.

"Could be, but it seems a bit far-fetched to react like that," Ross replied thinking. They'd just reached the station when news broke of the stabbing at the jail. Details were sketchy though it appeared poor Eric had been attacked by another prisoner, who he managed to kill with his own knife.

"What are the chances that we visit that scumbag and suddenly he's involved in a murder?" Dave asked, Ross, picking up his phone and dialling the jail. After a ten-minute conversation, Dave and Ross got the low down on what had happened.

"So he's in hospital under guard, and the other guy's dead. Let's look at Brody's sheet, see what he was in for." Ross suggested, bringing up Brody's criminal record. Both men went over it seeing the guy was an ex-fighter with a string of assaults and he liked young men.

"I think Eric's story is starting to look shaky. Like why would a guy that big need to protect himself with a knife? He could've snapped Eric in half, so why'd Eric kill him?" Dave mused.

"How long's he got before parole?" Ross asked.

"Just 24 months to go. So it can't be an escape after serving eight years inside." Dave replied.

"I don't get it. Somehow it's connected to that gun. I can feel it." Ross sensed trouble, but there was something he couldn't put his finger on.

"Well let's call it a night. We'll work it out tomorrow." Dave smiled glad to be heading home.

Twelve stitches and a pint of blood, found Eric spending the night at the hospital. It was normal to keep him there overnight to make sure there were no complications. Handcuffed to the bed and with two guards outside his room, Eric recovering waited. The two guards assigned to guard him took the job less than serious. Knowing he was handcuffed and injured, the guards relaxed talking to the many nurses who passed the bored guards.

Since the fight had been a spur of the moment thing no one considered he called for help. When the two surgeons in theatre gear, wearing facemasks came down the hallway, pushing a bed, neither guard gave them more than a passing glance. This was until one of them pulled a sawn-off shotgun out from under the pillow.

Taken by surprise, the two guards were forced into Eric's room, where they were bound and gagged before Eric put the boot into both of them. Without a word spoken by his rescuers, Eric was freed and placed on the bed and wheeled outside. Driving away in a stolen ambulance, Eric broke into laughter with his sons about how easy it had been.

"What now dad, do we take care of Michael?" Paul one of his sons asked smiling.

"No, not yet. I've got out to get my money back first. Killing him won't do that. No, once he repays the money, then I'll take care of that bastard. For now, I'm going to give him a lesson he won't forget." Eric smiled.

"Won't this affect your getting out in a year?" Steven his other son asked.

"I'll say, two friends, who thought I might be attacked again, broke me out. Being unconscious I didn't know what was happening till I woke the next day. Realising what they'd done, I turned myself in straight away. If I'm lucky, it shouldn't add more than a couple of months to my sentence. Anyway, it's worth it to get that money back." Eric confessed, looking forward to his time with Michael.

An hour after the escape Dave's phone rang. Grafton prison officers, seeing Dave had visited Eric that day, rung him. Asking him what they had discussed with the prisoner, seeing if there was a connection, they informed him what had happened. Looking at the clock, Dave saw it was close to nine. Since the escape was at 8, it meant if they were heading this way, they'd take another hour to arrive, even speeding, which they wouldn't he thought. Telling them it was a routine interview into an ongoing investigation, he assured them he'd alert the local police. Hanging up, Dave asked himself the big question, was what was going on?

Ringing Ross, he told him he'd pick him up in ten minutes. Throwing on his clothes from that day, he gave his wife and girls a quick kiss, racing out the door. Ross was waiting for him as he pulled up.

"The local boys are watching for him, what are we going to do?" Ross asked perplexed.

"He's broken out for a reason Ross. No one skips jail when they're a short-timer unless it's important." Dave pointed out.

"I thought about it all afternoon, even went over Eric's record. You know hardly any of his loot was ever recovered!" Ross informed him.

"Fuck do you think Michael found the money and the gun?" Dave put forward.

"It fits. Where did Michael get the money for his farm? He's supposed to have won it on the ponies!" Ross smiled. Dave putting the car into gear flattened it, hitting the siren. "Where are we going?" Ross asked surprised by his speed.

"Michael's, it's the only thing that makes sense!"

"Then turn the siren off. We don't want to spook anyone." Ross suggested, as Dave agreeing, killed it.

Michael and his friends sat on their front veranda listening to the radio enjoying the evening. Since the detectives visit, he'd been on edge, worrying about the gun. By now his father knew he'd taken the gun and the money and to put it lightly he was concerned. Telling the others, who already had enough to worry about with the cops finding the bodies, he found them unfazed. Like they'd told him, his father wouldn't be released for another two years when that date got closer, then they'd worry.

Their main concern was the investigation into Clark and Davison. Bella suspected the detective who liked her named Ross, was onto them. Michael felt the ground moving under him, his outlook on life fast turning pessimistic. Fate was closing in on him, and there was nothing he could do. Jed opposite watched Michael. He could see he was tense and who could blame him. He knew Michael had used up most of his reserve of money on him, keeping him supplied with drugs, prolonging his life. All that he had left now was the farm, and you just couldn't pack up and take it with you, when his father came looking.

Unbeknown to the others, Jed had been to see a doctor, as he'd had trouble sleeping. His doctor, who'd been looking after him since his release from jail, knew his condition well. Checking his vitals and his latest blood test, the doctor had become unusually silent, avoiding looking him in the eye. Jed knew he was coming to the end of the road, just by his look. In the end, the doctor had told him, roughly a year. Afterwards, he didn't know if he was upset or not, he only knew the suffering would soon be over. Leaving his friends was the only thing he'd miss he realised, hoping there was some type of hereafter for a druggie like him.

Kirra sitting next to Michael put on a brave face. She couldn't stand to be alone now; the thought of someone abusing her again filled her dreams with horror. Sometimes it was her uncle attacking her, other times it was Clark or Davison. No matter who it was, their perverted taste always seemed to fill her dreams with terror, making her dread going to sleep. Like Jed, she could see Michael was on edge, and who could blame him. The world was closing in on them again, and like before no one cared.

Bella of the four was oblivious to the others' worries. Since the night of her torture and rape, every day was special to her now. She knew she didn't talk freely like she once had, chattering on for hours on any subject. Now she liked to just listen, revelling in companionship, basking in the love she received from her friends. She knew she couldn't live without them; they were her heart and soul, part of her very being. Seeing the group was getting morose, Bella smiling turned up the radio.

Changing the channel, she searched for some dance music to get them moving. Instead, a news bulletin ground out its bland warning of a prisoner on the run, naming him. The group seemed to freeze, as they all looked to Michael. His face appeared to age ten years, as the colour left it, tears starting to cascade down his cheeks.

"He's coming for me!" Michael anguished voice moaned his lonely miserable childhood, coming back to crush him. "We've got to get out of here." He stammered out, becoming agitated, jumping to his feet.

"Settle down Michael, we don't know for sure." Jed tried to calm him. Unable to add anything else Michael stood gazing into the night, as Kirra standing pulled him to her comforting him.

"He's right, we've got to go." Kirra cried, leading Michael inside. Throwing anything they thought they'd need into bags, the four friends rushed to Michael's Ute. Starting it up Michael swung the car down their entry drive accelerating. They were halfway down the driveway when a car appeared at the entry to their farm blocking the road.

"It's them!" Michael screamed in panic. Swinging the car off the road, he drove several hundred metres into their paddocks, before the vehicle became bogged. "Run for it. I'll stay." Michael sobbed, not wanting his friends to be hurt, as he turned to confront his father. Dark, threatening figures could be seen approaching swiftly through the darkness, making him wish he'd run as well. Michael, turning to check on his friends found them standing with him, Jed holding a tyre lever.

"We won't leave you, Michael," Bella whispered as the four friends moved closer together preparing themselves. Strengthened by their support Michael heard his name yelled from the darkness.

"Michael it's the police! Stay where you are," Echoed the voice of Detective Johnson. The two detectives could now be seen approaching, their guns drawn. "Someone want to tell me, what's bloody well going on?" Dave demanded, looking the group over, as silence descended.

"It's funny Jed. For once you look glad to see us." Ross smiled.

"You just scared us, that's all." Jed murmured.

"So when you get scared by a car driving in your driveway, your response is to panic and get your own car bogged. Not very clever." Dave pointed out, as silence descended on the group.

"Wouldn't have anything to do with your old man escaping from jail tonight, would it?" Ross asked.

"Detective we heard it on the radio. We just thought he might try to hurt Michael." Kirra answered.

"Why would you be scared of him?" Dave asked, he was about to follow up with a question about Michael's race win at the track, when he saw for a brief second, the lights of a car pull up on the other side of Michael's property, before extinguishing.

"Everyone, back to the house," Dave whispered, pointing at the light.

"It's them." Michael murmured his body shaking.

"Yes it is Michael, and with your help, we can stop it here. Let's go." Dave ordered, leading the group back to the veranda. Ross following called for backup.

Reaching the house, Dave told Michael and Kirra to stay on the veranda, and pretend nothing was wrong, while Ross with Bella and Jed stayed out of sight inside. Ross would remain hidden out on the farm until Eric arrived. Dave knew they'd been lucky. If Eric had arrived earlier, he'd have seen them in the paddock near the road and pissed off. Now it was pitch dark, and by the time they made their way to Michael's house, their police car would be indistinguishable. Watching Michael and Kirra from inside, he wondered if the two could pull it off. Both to him appeared scared shitless.

Kirra sitting next to Michael felt him trembling. She too was on the verge of crying, as the darkness around them seemed to close in, smothering them. Pulling Michael to her, she wrapped a blanket around them both, hiding them. As they lay there on the lounge, their shape gave the impression of two lovers enjoying the night. 'Good girl' Dave thought seeing how Kirra had taken control, pulling Michael down on top of her, making the bait look more enticing.

In the dark not twenty metres away, Eric stood with Paul watching Michael with his woman. Taking the sawn-off shotgun from his son, Eric grinning, advanced onto the veranda. Michael looking down at Kirra was about to kiss her when he saw her eyes suddenly stare at something behind him. Turning, he saw his father come into the light.

"Well, well, well, if it isn't my little bastard son." Eric smiled, holding the gun pointing it at Michael.

"What are you doing here?" Michael managed to get out, all the time waiting for Detective Johnson to appear.

"You took something that didn't belong to you. I want it back." Eric demanded his eyes drawn to Kirra's legs. "Tell you what; while you think about it, I'll screw that little tart of yours. Show her what a man really can do. Mind you I've been inside for a while, might have to give her more than one go to get it right." Eric laughed, Paul, joining in. Kirra her nightmare becoming a reality broke down sobbing.

"Drop the gun, Eric!" Dave ordered coming out onto the veranda, causing both Eric and Paul to freeze. Eric still held the sawn-off shotgun in his hands, the barrel was still pointing towards Michael.

"I can still kill him copper, before you get me." Eric smiled, as Ross came up behind him.

"You can, but I'll put a hole in Paul, and you'll never get what you're after, will you?" Ross pointed out, his gun touching Paul's head. Eric stood between the two cops, as indecision made him hesitate. Killing Michael meant he'd lose the money. He didn't care if they shot Paul, but he'd lose his help in any future attempt to escape. Reluctantly he dropped the gun. Handcuffing Paul, Ross then handcuffed Eric, while Dave covered him, never taking his eyes off him.

"There'll be another time you little bastard." Eric spat out, making Michael and Kirra shrink back.

"By the time you get out Eric, he'll be in a retirement home," Dave assured him.

"What for escaping, I'll be lucky to get another two years." Eric laughed.

"You're being charged with murder as well as escaping," Dave informed him, wiping his smile off his face.

"It was self-defence." Eric snarled.

"Unfortunately for you, one of Brody's bum chums, saw you do it. You're fucked." Dave smiled, pushing Eric over. With his hands cuffed, he landed face first in the dirt.

Moments later, two police cars arrived. One contained Eric's other son Steven. They'd picked him up still sitting in their car at the property's boundary. After the uniformed cops had taken Eric and his sons away, Ross and Dave stayed to talk with Michael and his friends.

"You should be okay now Michael, though we'll be back in a couple of days to clear up certain matters," Dave informed him. Michael, looking broken and still shaken by what had just occurred, lifelessly nodded his head.

"Yes, it does worry us that your dad went to so much trouble, to come here to see you. Especially after we showed him that shotgun that you said you'd hadn't seen." Ross added.

"I don't know anything" Michael pleaded.

"Okay, we'll give you some time to pull yourself together. But when we come next time Michael, have a better story for us." Dave suggested.

Driving back to the station Dave wondered if they should've brought Michael in. He'd been through a lot, but the evidence against him was growing.

"You know Ross, I suspect Michael had that gun, and someone back there killed Davison and Clark. I'm sure they had their reasons, but sooner or later we have to find out." Dave told him. Ross' face showed grief, Dave realised he'd become too close.

"They've been through enough Dave. Be buggered if I'll do anything against the people who killed those two butchers." Ross replied, his knuckles turning white, as they gripped the wheel.

"That's not our call, mate. You know that."

"Okay, but I'll handle it, Dave," Ross assured him going silent for the rest of the journey to the station.

Back at the farm, Jed and Bella tried to calm Michael and Kirra. The night had overwhelmed what emotional barriers they had built up. Since the night Clark and Davison had come for them they all felt the pressure building on their stability. As the police cars disappeared into the night, the confused and frightened group moved inside. Barricading Michael's bedroom, the four friends slept together, fearing to be alone, wondering what waited for them outside in the dark. Unable to sleep, Michael switched on a small bedroom light.

"What are we going to do Jed?" Michael whispered, seeking some guidance from his friend.

"I don't know Michael. Our whole world is spinning out of control." Jed whispered distantly.

"I think the cops are onto us!" Kirra admitted, her voice quivering, as the night's horror possessed her. Bella beside her hugged her like she would a small child.

"I'm going for a walk to the falls tomorrow," Jed announced as silence settled over the group.

"Has it come to that?" Bella murmured sounding unsure.

"I see nothing for us." Jed softly replied.

"I'm with you Jed," Michael whispered as the room collapsed into a tomb of indecision.

At six the next morning the group awoke. Saying nothing, they all dressed having a small breakfast in quiet contemplation. Walking out the front door, they didn't bother even locking it, all jumping into Michael's ute. Travelling to the old abandoned railway, they parked the car, starting their walk, leaving the keys in the ignition.

"I'm not going to walk to the falls too frightened to talk." Kirra exploded, as the group smiling, hugged each other, moving off enjoying their time together.

At eight the same morning Ross having had a sleepless night decided to drive out to Michael's farm and have it out with him. There was no way he was bringing them in if he could help it, but he had to do something. Like Dave had said if he didn't someone else would.

Arriving at the farm, he parked walking to the front door. Seeing it ajar he became alert drawing his weapon.

"Bella are you there?" He yelled listening. When no answer came, he cautiously entered. No one was there. Plates and breakfast cereals littered the kitchen and dining table. Ross' instincts told him something was wrong, as Bella and Kirra were fastidious in keeping the place clean. Grabbing his two-way radio, he contacted Dave.

At first, Dave thought Ross was overreacting, so to placate him, he drove out to the farm. Ross was sitting on the front porch gazing sadly out towards the hills.

"Bella's so much like my daughter Dave. It would kill me if something happened to her." Ross confessed wiping his eyes as his friend sat down next to him.

"Get a grip, Ross. We don't know if there's a problem yet. They might be off shopping for all we know." Dave put forward, though the place he had to admit looked dejected as if its heart had gone.

"They've panicked mate, we've pushed them to the limit." Anguish flowing out of Ross as he spoke.

"Well let's go find them then!" Dave suggested pulling out his radio.

Contacting the station, Dave had a message sent out to all vehicles giving them the description and license number of Michael's ute. Next, he went into the house looking for clues. Ross was first to notice all their walking shoes were gone, having noticed on a previous trip that the four had good quality walking gear. Sure they were still in the area, as the great majority of their clothing and belongings were here, they drove back to the station to organise a search.

They'd been at the station for an hour when the first break occurred. A general duties car had found their Ute near the old railway line. Having no one in the station that did any serious walking, Dave called three local camping gear stores. He enquired if any knew of walking tracks that were near the spot where the vehicle was found. Out of the three shops, only one knew the area.

He told him there were only two walks from that spot on the line. One went towards the coast; the other went up into the hills to Minyon Falls. Dave stood frozen looking at Ross. He remembered seeing several photos during their search at the farmhouse. They were of the four friends standing at the falls. They had looked so happy. Ross next to him saw Dave's eyes as he was told the information. He knew what was coming.

"They've gone to the falls up in the range."

"Any chance there's a car in the area?" Ross' asked hopefully.

"No mate, the area is too isolated."

Instead of answering, Ross grabbed his car keys, running for the door. Dave silently followed him, as a feeling of hopelessness settled on him.

"Get the fuck out of the way!" Dave yelled from his window as Ross swerved onto the wrong side of the road passing the dickhead. It never failed to amaze him how stupid drivers could be. A police car comes screaming up behind them, sirens and lights going full tilt and they freeze in the middle of the road, wondering what to do. This was the third car they'd been forced around since they'd left the station. Mind you they were doing close to one hundred and seventy in an eighty zone. No surprise then that the people were startled.

They'd been driving like crazy for over an hour along old dirt roads, used once by tree hauliers carving out the forest. Now the whole area was a National Park, full of slow-moving tourists. Ross hadn't said much since they left, obsessed with finding Bella. Watching him, Dave could see the strain of finding out what had happened to his daughter and now this was pushing him over the edge.

"We'll get there in time Ross don't worry," Dave reassured him, scared of what would happen to his friend if they didn't.

"It's a long walk, they would've rested, but it's going to be close.' Ross answered his voice cracking under strain. Dave for the thousandth time thought he should be driving, wondering how close Ross was to losing it.

MINYON FALLS

The four friends without a word dressed, preparing for the last section of their walk. Leaving the Billabong, they walked along an old track holding each other's hands. Even though the falls were still ten minute's walk, the distant sound of the water thundering over the falls echoed through the bushland thundering against their chests. Jed looked sideways at Bella to see tears running down her cheeks. She ambled along as if sleepwalking, her chest jerking as she sobbed soundlessly.

Kirra too had tears on her cheeks, as each of them silently contemplated what they were about to do.

Reaching the fence area next to the falls Michael gazed out over the valley. "God it's beautiful here," he thought, squeezing Kirra's hand reassuringly. The heavy rains over the last week had turned the falls from a trickle to a raging torrent. Most times in the past when they'd been here, they'd walked across planks of wood secured on the tops of massive stones. The planks weaved their way across the falls right next to the edge. Now only the very tops of the timbers could be seen, and they were covered by slippery mud.

"Watch your step. You wouldn't want to slip." Michael warned without thinking, as his friends burst into laughter at his blunder. The laughter soon faded, as the friends embraced each other, holding and kissing as all of them broke down and cried.

"Let's go," Jed whispered, moving out onto the walkway, as Bella followed him holding his hand. Michael came next supporting Kirra, who was scared of heights of all things. Reaching the middle the four turned facing the valley.

"I can't do this Jed!" Bella screamed above the noise as Jed smiled back. He'd known since the Billabong that

Bella's belief would stop her. He wasn't upset by this, having always admired her faith in her God.

"That's okay Bella I've always loved you for the person you are. I'll be waiting for you." He yelled smiling, as she hugged him crying. Ross screaming interrupted their goodbye, as his arms enclosed both of them.

As they neared the falls, Ross turned off the sirens and lights as to not startle them. Passing a lookout across from the falls, Dave saw no one there.

"We beat them!" Dave smiled as Ross covered the last two kilometres in record time. Both men jumped from their car running to the falls to see the group walking out onto the plank walkway.

"Take it easy!" Dave yelled to Ross, as seeing Bella he sprinted to the walkway. Dave having no choice, ran after him. Michael and Kirra were closer, so as Ross came up to them, he grabbed hold, passing them to Dave. Moving on, he leapt to Bella and Jed who were holding each other, Bella sobbing.

"I'm here Jenny!" Ross screamed grabbing the two securing them in a bear hug.

Behind him Dave led Michael and Kirra off the walkway, handcuffing them through a railing. He then turned to help Ross. Heights had never been Dave's strong point. As he inched out to where Ross held Jed and Bella, he tried to focus on his friend and not look down. When the cracking noise started, Dave froze.

Looking down at the timber he was standing on, he saw that it appeared stable. Relieved he looked back towards Ross, Jed and Bella, they were gone. Looking again, he saw the three in the turbulent water, hanging on to what was left of the timber plank. Somehow when the timber they were standing on broke in two, the side away from Dave had become lodged on one of its remaining bolts. It had swung sideways with the three of them, their feet metres from the edge of the falls.

The timber walkway was never meant to hold back a raging torrent of water, while supporting three people. Going swiftly with a loud crack, both Jed and Ross had grabbed onto what was left of the bridge, while at the same time hanging on to Bella. Where Ross found the strength from, Dave would never know, as he slowly pulled Bella up over him, onto the small piece of timber. Jed feeling Ross taking the load also crawled up over Ross making it onto the timber, next to Bella. Both now reached back for Ross, grabbing a hand each.

"Let me go! Save yourselves!" He screamed, happy he'd saved his girl.

"No!" Bella screamed, refusing to let him go, as the bolt holding the timber gave up its fight, breaking loose. The three knowing they were doomed, quickly pulled each other close, as they disappeared from view.

Dave beside them watched it happen as if it was in slow motion. The three huddled together looked towards him, fear written on their faces, as Bella in desperation, started to scream. Unable to reach them, Dave cringed back as their screams echoed over the valley walls. The sound of their voices slowly dissipated as they plunged down the side of the water-covered cliff.

"No!" Dave moaned, holding his face in his hands shocked. Wiping his eyes, he slowly backed away from the falls. Looking at the other two, he quickly pulled himself together.

"One of them could still be alive, let's go!" He shouted releasing them from the handcuffs.

Driving back towards the lookout, where a path led down to the base of the falls, Dave called for backup. He requested an ambulance and a rescue team, plus any police in the area. Reaching the lookout, he jumped out of his car, running down to the start of the track. Seeing

Michael and Kirra were following, he proceeded down the steep trail, coming out on a flat area below the falls.

Running like a madman, he called out Ross' name, again and again, hoping for a miracle. It wasn't to be. Turning a corner, he saw the three bloodied bodies, face down, floating together in a pool below the falls. Running to the pool, Michael and Dave dived in, swimming to their friends. Finding the water was only shoulder deep, they pulled the bodies back to the shore. Dave checked each one having trouble looking at his dead partner shredded face. Kirra crying uncontrollably, helped pull the bodies out of the water.

Crumbling to the ground, Dave broke down, unable to do anything but cry. Two pairs of hands held him, as Michael and Kirra sat beside him, mourning the passing of their friends.

The sound of approaching voices shouting broke the three out of their grief. Dave standing wiped his face. Looking at his watch, it came to him that he'd made the call for backup over three hours ago. Kirra and Michael still hadn't said a word; they still sat dejected on the ground.

"Let me do the talking." He whispered as the State Emergency service with several police officers came into view.

"My God! Is that Detective Luke?" One of the police officers asked, staring at the bodies, as the SES men handed Dave, Kirra and Michael a blanket.

"He tried to stop Jed from jumping. Bella was with him trying to talk her boyfriend out of taking the leap when the timber walkway gave way. There was nothing anyone could've done." Dave told them, looking at Kirra and Michael.

"What about these two?" Another officer asked.

"They came with Bella, they helped me come down here and pull them out of the water," Dave answered, his voice breaking. The men grew quiet seeing the stress and grief that Dave was under.

"Best you three go, we'll bring them up." The SES officer suggested softly, as Dave helped Michael and Kirra to their feet. Ambling up the trail the three held each other's hand for support, all feeling the loss.

"How do you recover from something like this?" They heard a voice behind them ask, as silently the three climbed up the steep track to the lookout. Already a crowd was gathering, as word got out about the deaths at the falls. Two officers left at the lookout, moved the people back, giving their detective and the two young people access to his vehicle. Once inside, he started the car, driving away. Halfway down the mountain road, Dave pulled over.

"Why kill yourselves?' Dave asked softly, looking back at Kirra and Michael in the rearview mirror.

"I killed the Doctor and the Dean at the farm, they came to kill Michael and me. They'd knocked Michael out and then tried to rape me." Kirra sobbed then continued. "They stripped me and threw me across the kitchen floor. I landed on the garbage bin; the gun was hidden in it. It fell out, and I grabbed it, pulling the triggers. The others helped me get rid of their bodies. We thought now with Michael's father after us as well, it was all over." Kirra sobbed.

Dave felt like screaming at them for being so stupid. Nothing came as he realised he'd been responsible for pushing them into this whole mess.

"Look there's no reason why you can't move and start over somewhere else. Sell the farm and move, get away from here. By the time Michael's old man gets out of jail, you'll be long gone."

"What about what we did?" Michael whispered sadly.

"No one gives a shit about who killed those two fucks. You did the world a favour. Now we've got to go to the station and make statements. I know it's hard, but you've got to back me up and say Jed did the shooting. You went there with Bella to try and stop him from killing himself. Understand?"

"What about dad's gun?"

"It's circumstantial Michael, forget about it. Just promise me one thing, no more of this bullshit, about doing yourselves in."

"Thanks, Dave." Was all Kirra could say before starting to sob again, as Michael held her. Dave knew it was enough.

THE PRESENT

Dave helped his wife down the steep section of the track, hoping he had the strength to climb back up. As the track widened, Helen reached across holding Dave's hand. I time they came to the base as of the waterfall. The water though thundering down wasn't as mind-numbing as that day ten years ago. Walking to the side of the pond, Dave saw the monument placed here for Ross' bravery and for the remembrance of Jed and Bella still stood untouched by the elements.

Helen seeing Dave was lost in thought moved forward placing a small bunch of flowers at the base of the monument. Moving away towards the cliff, Dave sat down on a seat, made out of pieces of rock, cemented into a bench. Helen sitting down beside him held his hand, as Dave continued to stare down the valley.

"This is my last visit old friend." Dave sadly announced, looking at the pond. Age had finally beaten him, he knew he'd be lucky to get back up that track, let alone visit again.

"He understands Dave, you were his best friend," Helen assured him.

His answer, if he had one, was drowned by the sound of playful screaming as two young children ran into sight. It was followed by a father's shout to keep away from the water, as a bearded man in his late thirties appeared catching up to them.

"Don't go near the water or run ahead again, you scared your mother," The man shouted, spotting Dave and Helen. "I'm sorry I didn't see you two sitting there. Hope they didn't disturb you?"

"That's okay. One of our daughters has kids too. They can be a handful." Helen laughed.

"Yes, Jed and Bella can be a handful sometimes." The man answered as Dave who'd been watching the two children came to life.

"Did you say, Jed and Bella?" Dave croaked out standing up. Turning around to look down the track, he saw the woman gasp her hands going to her mouth.

"Dave!' She cried running forward hugging him. The children, Helen and the man, stood spellbound. Feeling faint, Dave dropped back down onto the bench, as the woman continued to hug him, going to her knees.

"Then this must be Michael?" Dave sobbed, as Michael came towards him. Shaking his hand he sat down beside him, hugging him too. Helen seeing something special was happening, walked over to the kids taking their hands.

"Want to come exploring?" She asked offering her hands, as the two children excitedly agreed, leading them around the falls.

"I can't believe you're here." Dave sobbed, wiping his nose, trying to pull himself together.

"We brought the children to show them where we once lived. We thought while here, we'd pay our respects." Michael explained, standing. Looking at him, Dave saw the skinny young boy was gone, replaced by a solid built confident-looking man. Kirra too had changed, she still was beautiful, but more mature, more in control.

"You know I followed your lives for a couple of years after you left here. Last time I checked, around four years ago, you were in Queensland near Rockhampton. After that, I'm afraid I stopped checking." Dave admitted.

"Yes, we stayed there for a couple of years, before moving on. We made several attempts at putting down roots since leaving here. In the end, we found what we were looking for in the Margaret River area in WA. There we bought a small vineyard, we've been there growing grapes ever since." Michael answered as Kirra squeezed his hand.

"It was funny ending up back again on the land. Somehow we have always been drawn to it." Kirra reflected, her eyes betraying the underlying pain of what occurred on Michael's first farm.

"I'll have to come one day and hit you up for a free drink." Dave decided to move on.

"You will always be welcome to stay with us." Kirra smiled wiping her eyes.

Helen soon arrived back with the two children. After Kirra and Michael had their time with their departed friends, they headed back to the lookout. Dave had never felt better, as he and Helen worked their way back up to the lookout, assisted by Kirra and Michael. Driving back to Dave's place they talked Kirra and Michael into staying the night, catching up, before reluctantly they had to leave the next day.

Giving their address in Western Australia to Dave and Helen, Kirra made them promise to visit. Assuring them, they would, a stillness settled over the four. Kirra and Michael's children, unaffected by the moment, squealed delightedly at the start of another travel adventure. As the children rushed to their seats, the adults said their goodbyes, exchanging hugs.

Standing on the front driveway, Dave happily waved goodbye to Kirra and Michael. He was also waving goodbye to those tragic memories from his past, his thoughts went back to the falls. 'Ross you didn't die in vain,' he smiled, as the honking of a horn announced the arrival of his two daughters. In their twenties, one married, with two boys, both still lived on the coast south of Byron.

"Who was that?" Kristyn the oldest and the one married asked, having seen their parents waving.

"Just some old friends who dropped by," Dave replied. He didn't want to go into detail at the moment.

"What brings you to here so early?" Helen asked as they all moved inside, Helen, putting on the jug, boiling water for a cuppa.

"Nothing serious, I just wanted dad's advice on something." Kim smiled, before giggling.

"What is so funny?" Dave asked, wondering why they'd asked for advice now since they hadn't listened in the past twenty years.

"Scaredy cat here thought she saw a shadow at the window of her unit last night. Screamed the house down, had all the neighbours, including us, into a search for her mysterious shadow." Kristyn laughed, Kim, looking embarrassed.

"Well, it scared me, whatever it was," Kim answered. "What do you think I should do dad?"

The room lapsed into silence as Dave started to cry.

THE END

www.ingramcontent.com/pod-product-compliance
Lightning Source LLC
Chambersburg PA
CBHW031245120726
47905CB00002B/732